P9-BZM-326

KAREN HESSE

Letters from Rifka

HAMPTON-BROWN

THE EXCHANGE

What is the best way to survive hard times?

From *Letters from Rifka*. Text copyright © 1992 by Karen Hesse.
Reprinted by arrangement with Henry Holt and Company, LLC.

Cover illustration from *Letters from Rifka* by Karen Hesse, illustration by Diana Zelvin. Cover illustration copyright © 1993 by Diana Zelvin. Cover design by Patricia Isaza. Reprinted by permission of Penguin Young Readers Group, a member of Penguin Group (USA) Inc.

Poems from *The Works of Alexander Pushkin* by Alexander Pushkin edited by Avraham Yarmolinsky, copyright © 1936 and renewed 1964 by Random House, Inc. Used by permission of Modern Library, a division of Random House, Inc.

On-Page Coach™ (introductions, questions, on-page glossaries),
The Exchange, back cover summary © Hampton-Brown.

All rights reserved. No part of this book may be reproduced or transmitted in any form or by any means, electronic or mechanical, including photocopying, recording, or by any information storage and retrieval system, without permission in writing from the publisher.

Hampton-Brown
P.O. Box 223220
Carmel, California 93922
800-333-3510
www.hampton-brown.com

Printed in the United States of America

ISBN-13: 978-0-7362-2791-9
ISBN-10: 0-7362-2791-1

13 14 15 16 10 9 8 7 6 5

Acknowledgments

The author wishes to acknowledge the assistance of the following people, whose counsel and expertise contributed to the body and soul of this work: Applied Graphics; Lucille Avrutin; Betsey Bonin and the Book Cellar; Eileen Christelow; Esther Evenson; Beverly Fischel; Ethel Gelfand; Randy, Kate, and Rachel Hesse; Sandra King and the Brooks Memorial Library; Randy, Ronny, and Marni Letzler; Fran Levin; Robert MacLean; Bernice Millman; Liza Ketchum Murrow; Cynthia Nau and the Moore Free Library; Howard Sacks; Arlyn Sharpe; Society of Children's Book Writers/ Newfane chapter—in particular, Winifred Bruce Luhrmann, Cynthia Stowe, Michael Waite, and Nancy Hope Wilson; Starr Library at Middlebury College; Vermont Southeast Regional Library: Amy Howlett, Gwendolyn Jennings, Joan Knight, Deborah Tewksbury, and Sophia Wessel; and Kevin Weiler.

With special thanks to Brenda Bowen and Barbara Kouts.

*In memory of
Zeyde and Bubbe,
my beloved grandparents*

Author's Note

When I began this book, I set out to write about my family's migration from Russia to the United States. I recalled a story about my grandmother wearing white kid gloves as she rode through Poland in the back of an oxcart. I remembered the tale of my grandfather, denied passage on the *Titanic* because he was "only an immigrant." But that's all I remembered.

I phoned my mother and my aunts for help. They contributed a wealth of stories about their own childhood, but they couldn't shed much light on the family history.

"Call your great-aunt Lucy," my mother suggested.

I barely remembered Aunt Lucy. I pictured a frail, eighty-year-old woman. To my surprise, the voice on the other end of the line resounded with strength, steadiness, and humor.

"Certainly I'll help you," she said. "What do you want to know?"

I sent Aunt Lucy a list of questions in the mail. She shot me back a tape on which she spoke at breakneck speed for five breathless minutes. I remember holding on to the handle of my tape player, feeling like a passenger on a roller coaster as I listened to Aunt

Lucy's account of her journey to America. When she signed off, the hiss and crackle of blank tape taunted me.

I phoned Aunt Lucy again. "I've listened to your tape," I said. "I think I need to see you."

She laughed as if she'd known I was coming all along.

Two months later, on a steamy East Coast afternoon, with my head full of research, I arrived on Aunt Lucy's doorstep.

Greeting me was a tiny woman with an unruly bun of snow-white hair on the top of her head. She welcomed me into her home and into her past.

Letters from Rifka draws largely on the memories of Lucy Avrutin. I have changed names and adjusted certain details, but this story is, above all else, Aunt Lucy's story.

BEFORE YOU MOVE ON...

1. **Author's Purpose** Why did the author call Aunt Lucy?

2. **Genre** This story is based on fact, but it is fiction. How do you know?

LOOK AHEAD Read pages 7–13 to find out who tells the story of Rifka's escape from Russia.

Rifka writes a letter to her cousin about her family's escape from Russia. Rifka distracts the guards at the train station while her family gets on the train.

. . . and from
The gloomy land of lonely exile
To a new country bade me come. . . .
—Pushkin

September 2, 1919
Russia

My Dear Cousin Tovah,
 We made it! If it had not been for your father,
though, I think my family would all be dead now:
Mama, Papa, Nathan, Saul, and me. At the very
best we would be in that filthy prison in Berdichev,
not rolling west through Ukraine on a freight train
bound for Poland.

....

We made it! We left Russia!
If it had not been for your father If your father did not help us
bound for going to

I am sure you and Cousin Hannah were glad to see Uncle Avrum come home today. How worried his daughters must have been after the locked doors and whisperings of last night.

Soon Bubbe Ruth, my dear little grandmother, will hear of our escape. I hope she gives a big pot of Frusileh's cream to Uncle Avrum. How better could she thank him?

When the sun rose above the trees at the train station in Berdichev this morning, I stood alone outside a boxcar, my heart **knocking against my ribs**.

I stood there, trying to look older than my twelve years. Wrapped in the new shawl Cousin Hannah gave to me, still I trembled.

"Wear this in health," Hannah had whispered in my ear as she draped the shawl over my shoulders early this morning, before we slipped from your house into the dark.

"Come," Papa said, leading us through the woods to the train station.

I looked back to the flickering lights of your

---

knocking against my ribs beating fast

house, Tovah.

"Quickly, Rifka," Papa whispered. "The boys, and Mama, and I must hide before light."

"You can distract the guards, can't you, little sister?" Nathan said, putting an arm around me. In the darkness, I could not see his eyes, but I **felt them studying me**.

"Yes," I answered, not wanting to disappoint him.

At the train station, Papa and Mama hid behind bales of hay in boxcars to my right. My two giant brothers, Nathan and Saul, **crouched** in separate cars to my left. Papa said that we should hide in different cars. If the guards discovered only one of us, perhaps the others might still escape.

Behind me, in the dusty corner of a boxcar, sat my own **rucksack**. It waited for me, holding what little I own in this world. I had packed Mama's candlesticks, wrapped in my two heavy dresses, at the bottom of the sack.

Your gift to me, the book of Pushkin, I did not

---

felt them studying me knew he was looking closely at me
crouched bent down
rucksack backpack

pack. I kept it out, holding it in my hands.

I would have liked to fly away, to race back up the road, stopping at every door to say good-bye, to say that we were going to America.

But I could not. Papa said we must tell no one we were leaving, not even Bubbe Ruth. Only you and Hannah and Uncle Avrum knew. I'm so glad at least you knew, Tovah.

As Papa expected, not long after he and Mama and the boys had hidden themselves, two guards **emerged** from a wooden shelter. They **thundered down** the platform in their heavy boots, climbing in and out of the cars, making their search.

They did not notice me at first. Saul says I am too little for anyone to notice, but you know Saul. He never has a nice word to say to me. And I am small for a girl of twelve. Still, my size did not keep the guards from noticing me. I think the guards missed seeing me at first because they were so busy in their search of the train. They were searching for Nathan.

---

emerged came out
thundered down walked loudly on

You know as well as I, Tovah, that when a Jewish boy **deserts** the Russian Army, the army tries hard to find him. They bring him back and kill him in front of his regiment as a warning to the others. Those who have helped him, they also die.

Late last night, when Nathan **slipped away** from his regiment and appeared at our door, joy filled my heart at seeing my favorite brother again. Yet a troubled look worried Nathan's face. He hugged me only for a moment. His dimpled smile vanished as quickly as it came.

"I've come," he said, "to warn Saul. The soldiers will soon follow. They will take him into the army."

I am ashamed, Tovah, to admit that at first hearing Nathan's news made me glad. I wanted Saul gone. He **drives me crazy**. From his big ears to his big feet, I cannot stand the sight of him. Good riddance, I thought.

How foolish I was not to understand what Nathan's news really meant to our family.

....

deserts suddenly leaves
slipped away escaped
drives me crazy bothers me

"You should not have come," Mama said to Nathan. "They will shoot you when you return."

Papa said, "Nathan isn't going to return. Hurry! We must pack!"

We all stared at him.

"Quickly," Papa said, clapping his hands. "Rifka, run and fill your rucksack with all of your belongings." I do not know what Papa thought I owned.

Mama said, "Rifka, do you have room in your bag for my candlesticks?"

"The candlesticks, Mama?" I asked.

"We either take them, Rifka, or leave them to the greedy peasants. Soon enough they will **swoop down like vultures to pick our house bare**," Mama said.

Papa said, "Your brothers in America have sent for us, Rifka. It is time to leave Russia and we are not coming back. Ever."

"Don't we need **papers**?" I asked.

Papa looked from Nathan to Saul. "There is no

....

swoop down like vultures to pick our house bare
take everything in our house

papers passports; travel documents

time for papers," he said.

Then I began to understand.

We huddled in your cellar through the black night, planning our escape. Uncle Avrum **only shut you out** to protect you, Tovah.

Hearing the guards speak this morning, I understood his precaution. It was dangerous enough for you to know we were leaving. We could not risk telling you the details of our escape in case the soldiers came to question you.

....

only shut you out did not tell you what was happening

BEFORE YOU MOVE ON...

1. **Narrator** Rifka is telling this story. How does she tell the story?

2. **Conflict** Rifka's brother Nathan tried to leave the Russian Army. Why did this cause the family to leave Russia?

LOOK AHEAD Read pages 14–27 to find out if Rifka can help her family escape.

The guards were talking about Nathan. They were saying what they would do to him once they found him, and what they would do to anyone who had helped him.

Nathan hid under a stack of burlap bags, one boxcar away from me. I knew, no matter how frightened I was, I must not let them find Nathan.

The guards said terrible things about our family. They did not know me, or Mama or Papa. They did not even know Nathan, not really. They could never have said those things about my brother Nathan if they knew him. Saul, maybe, clumsy-footed Saul. They could have said hateful things about Saul, but never Nathan. The guards **spoke ill of** us, not because of anything we had done, not because of anything we had said. Just because we were Jews. Why is it, Tovah, that in Russia, **no matter what the trouble, the blame always falls upon the Jews**?

The guards' bayonets plunged into bales and bags and crates in each boxcar. That is how they searched,

....

spoke ill of said bad things about

no matter what the trouble, the blame always falls upon the Jews everyone thinks the Jews cause all the problems

The guards' bayonets plunged The guards used rifles with knives to cut with the brutal blades of their bayonets. The sound of steel in wood echoed through the morning.

I stood trembling in the dawn, Tovah, gripping your book in my hands to steady myself. I feared the guards would guess from one look at me what I was hiding.

For just a moment, I glanced toward the cars where Mama and Papa hid, to gather courage from them. My movement must have caught the guards' attention.

"You!" I heard a voice shout. "You there!"

The guards **hastened down the track** toward me. One had a rough, unshaven face and a broad mouth. He stared at me for a moment or two as if he recognized me. Then he seemed to change his mind. He reached out to touch my hair.

This is what Papa hoped for, I think. People have often stopped in wonder at my blond curls.

You say a girl must not **depend on her looks**, Tovah. It is better to be **clever**. But as the guards

....

hastened down the track hurried

depend on her looks think that being beautiful will help her get what she wants

clever smart

inspected me, from the worn toes of my boots to my hair spilling out from under my kerchief, I hoped my looks would be enough.

I hated the guard touching my hair. I clutched your book of poetry tighter to keep my hands from **striking him away**. I knew I must not anger him. If I angered him, I not only put my life in danger, I endangered Mama and Papa and Nathan and Saul, too.

The guard with the unshaven face held my curls in his hand. He looked **up and down the length of me** as if he were hungry and I were a piece of Mama's pastry. I held still. **Inside I twisted like a wrung rag**, but on the outside I held still.

Papa is so brave, the guards would not frighten him. I remember the time soldiers came to our house and saw on Papa's feet a new pair of boots. Uncle Shlomo had made them for Papa from leftover pieces of leather. The soldiers said, "Take the boots off. Give them here." Papa refused. The soldiers whipped Papa,

---

striking him away hitting him so that he would go away
up and down the length of me at me all over
Inside I twisted like a wrung rag I felt very nervous

but still Papa refused to hand over his boots. They would have killed Papa for those boots, but **their battalion** marched into sight. The soldiers hit Papa once more, hard, so that he spit blood, but they left our house empty-handed.

This was the courage of my papa, but how could he ever think I had such courage?

Courage or not, of all my family, only I could stand before the Russian soldiers, because of my blond hair and my blue eyes. Papa, Mama, and the boys, they all have the dark coloring and features of the Jews. Only I **can pass for** a Russian peasant.

And of course, as you know, Tovah, of all my family, only I can speak Russian without a Yiddish accent. Uncle Avrum calls it my "gift" for language. What kind of gift is this, Tovah?

The guard ran his greasy fingers through my curls. He smelled of **herring** and onion.

"Why aren't you on your way to school?" he demanded.

....

their battalion the other soldiers in their group
can pass for look like
herring fish

My heart beat in my throat where my voice should have been. Mama is always saying **my mouth is as big as the village well**. Even you, Tovah, tell me I should not speak unless I have something to say. I know I talk too much. Yet as the guard played with my hair, **fear silenced me**.

"Who are you?" he asked. "What are you doing here?"

I forced myself to answer. I spoke in Russian, making my accent just like Katya's, the peasant girl who comes to light our Sabbath fire.

"I'm here," I said, "to take the train. My mother has found me work in a wealthy house."

"You are young to leave home," the rough-faced guard said, brushing the ends of my hair across his palm. "And such a pretty little thing."

"That's just what I told my mother," I said. "But she **insisted that I** go anyway."

The guard laughed. "Maybe you should stay in Berdichev. I might have better work for you here."

....

my mouth is as big as the village well I talk too much
fear silenced me I was too afraid to speak
insisted that I said that I must

"Maybe I will," I said, looking into his rough, ugly face.

Papa did not tell me what to say to the guards. He simply said to distract them.

If it had been just the one guard, I might have **occupied him** until the train left the station.

Only there was another guard. He had a thin face and a straight back. His eyes were like the Teterev in the spring when the snow melts, churning with green ice. My curls did not interest him.

"Let her go," the thin guard ordered. "Search the boxcars around and behind her."

My heart banged in my throat.

I had to keep the guards away from my family until Uncle Avrum arrived from the factory. I prayed for Uncle Avrum to come soon.

Tovah, I tried to do what you are always telling me. I tried to be clever.

"You are in the army, aren't you?" I said. "I know all about soldiers in the army."

---

occupied him kept him busy

My heart banged in my throat. My heart beat so hard I felt it in my throat.

The guard with the eyes of green ice stared hard at me. "Tell me what you know," he demanded.

"Well," I said. "When I was nine, I saw some soldiers from Germany. Did you ever see those German soldiers?"

Both of the guards looked as if they remembered the Germans well.

"Those Germans came in airplanes," I said. "So noisy, those planes." I clasped my hands over my ears, banging myself with your book of Pushkin.

The stiff-backed guard **glared at me**.

"There was a German pilot," I said. "A German pilot with a big potbelly. I wondered how he could fit in his plane; such a small plane, such a big German."

The thin guard **pivoted** away from me. He **squinted** at something moving in the bushes across the train yard. Lifting his rifle, he aimed at the bushes and fired. Two birds rose noisily into the air.

I started talking faster.

"That German liked me pretty well," I said. "He

---

glared at me looked at me with anger
pivoted turned
squinted looked

bought me candy and took me for walks. One day he put me in his plane and started the propeller. I didn't like that, so I jumped out."

I knew I was talking too fast. When I talked like this at home, Saul always got annoyed with me.

I couldn't make myself slow down. **The words came spilling out.** If I could just keep them listening, they would run out of time to search the train.

"I jumped out of that fat German's plane and landed in the mud," I said. "And I ran home like the devil was chasing me. The German called for me to stop, but I wasn't stopping for him. I—"

"Enough!" the thin guard commanded. "Enough of your **chatter**." He pushed me aside and climbed into the freight car behind me. He sank his bayonet into the hay bales inside the car.

I asked the guard with the rough beard, "What is the problem? What is he looking for?" I tried to keep my voice from **betraying** my fear.

Suddenly the guard reappeared in the doorway to

....

The words came spilling out. I spoke very quickly.

chatter talking

betraying showing

the freight car with my rucksack dangling from his bayonet. "What is this?"

I thought, If he finds Mama's candlesticks in my rucksack, it is all over for my entire family. "I can't go without my belongings, can I?" I said.

The two guards started arguing.

"Leave the girl alone," said the one with the rough beard. "She's a peasant, **farmed out** by her mother."

The other narrowed his eyes. "She's hiding something," he said.

"What could she hide?"

The thin guard glared at me again. "This is very heavy for clothing," he said, swinging my rucksack at the end of his bayonet. "What have you got in here?"

"What do you think?" said the guard with the rough face. "You think she's hiding a Jew in her rucksack? You think she **has something to do with** the Nebrot boy? Look at her, listen to her. She's no Jew."

The other guard jumped down from the car, tossing my rucksack on the ground. My bag hit

....

farmed out told to leave home and go work
has something to do with is helping

with a **thud**.

"What's in there?" he asked again, preparing to rip my bag open with the razor-sharp blade of his bayonet.

"Books," I said. "Like this one." I held up your Pushkin, Tovah. "I like to read."

The guard hesitated, staring into my face, but he did not rip open my rucksack. He started instead toward the next car, the car with Nathan inside. I did not know how to stop him.

That is when your father arrived, Tovah. It had taken him longer at the factory than he'd expected.

"Guards! Come here!" Uncle Avrum shouted from the woods.

The guards turned toward his voice. I turned, too. The trees on either side of the road **dwarfed Uncle Avrum**. He stood short and round with his red beard brushing the front of his coat. I knew the smell of that coat.

He and Papa and Mama had planned for this. Mama had hoped not to involve your father, but

---

thud loud noise
dwarfed Uncle Avrum made Uncle Avrum seem smaller

Uncle Avrum insisted on **being part of the plan**. He would make certain the guards suspected nothing. He said Papa could not **let the fate of our entire family rest on the shoulders of a child**.

I did not like when he talked about me that way last night, calling me a child. I felt insulted. Yet when I heard him call out to the guards this morning, all I felt was relief.

"Guards!" Uncle Avrum shouted again. "My factory. Someone broke into my factory." He is a good actor, your father, in case you didn't know.

The guards squinted their eyes against the morning sun. They recognized Uncle Avrum, but the thin guard did not want to help him.

"We must **inspect** this entire train before it leaves the station," he said to the guard beside him. "That man is only a Jew. Why bother with the troubles of a Jew?"

The guard with the unshaven face hesitated. "We might get in trouble if we don't help him. That's Avrum Abromson. I once carried a message to him at

....

being part of the plan helping us

let the fate of our entire family rest on the shoulders of a child make me responsible for helping the family escape

inspect look at everyone on

his factory. He has important friends."

"Come!" Uncle Avrum demanded. "Hurry! I haven't got all day."

I thought they would shoot Uncle Avrum for speaking to them in that way. They certainly would have shot Papa. But Uncle Avrum's demand seemed to **make up their minds** to go with him. I knew your family had **influence**, Tovah, but I never realized how much. The guards left me by the train and headed across the **clearing** toward your father and his factory. I prayed Uncle Avrum had made the robbery look real so they would not **suspect him**.

The train whistle blew, once, twice, as the rough-bearded guard and Uncle Avrum disappeared up the road. The thin guard turned back toward me, looking for a moment as if he might change his mind and return to finish the inspection. Then he, too, vanished into the woods.

The train, straining on the tracks, moved a little backward before it started rolling forward, slowly, out of Berdichev.

....

make up their minds help them decide
influence power
clearing field
suspect him think that he helped us escape

You know what a good runner I am. I have learned to run to keep out of Saul's reach. Outrunning the train was easy. I heaved my rucksack from the ground, tossing it into the boxcar. Stones skipped out from under my boots as I **scrambled** alongside, jumped on board, and, sprawling on my belly, pulled myself in.

Quickly I **tucked into the shadows** of the car so no one could see me. The freight car smelled warm and rich, like cattle, and I thought of Bubbe Ruth's sweet cow Frusileh.

I write this letter to you with my good school pencil in the blank pages at the front of your Pushkin. I am writing very neat and tiny so as not to spoil the book. I hope you do not mind that I am writing in your book, Tovah, but I have no other paper. I know this letter can never reach you, but **in writing to you**, I feel less frightened. You have been a big sister and a best friend to me. I cannot bear to think of never talking to you again. So I will talk to you by writing about my journey.

....

scrambled ran
tucked into the shadows hid in the shadows
in writing to you when I write to you

We are heading for the Polish border. That is all I know. I cannot even speak the language. What will it be like in Poland, and beyond that, in America, where at last I will meet my three oldest brothers? I can hardly believe that I too will soon live in such a place as America.

Shalom, my little house. Shalom, my family; shalom, Berdichev, and my dear little grandmother, Bubbe Ruth. Shalom, Hannah and Aunt Anna and Uncle Avrum, but most of all Tovah,

Shalom to you,
Rifka

....

Shalom Good-bye; Peace (in Hebrew)

BEFORE YOU MOVE ON...

1. **Plot** How did Rifka save her family from the guards? Who else helped? How?

2. **Character** Why was Rifka chosen to distract the guards?

LOOK AHEAD Read pages 28–34 to find out what the doctor did when the train stopped in Poland.

Rifka's family rides the train to Poland. They are inspected by a doctor when they get there.

. . . And with a sword he clove my breast,
Plucked out the heart he made beat higher,
And in my stricken bosom pressed
Instead a coal of living fire. . . .
—Pushkin

ﻉ

September 3, 1919
Poland

Dear Tovah,

We were **fortunate** that we ran into no further trouble until we reached the Polish border. At the border, though, guards came **aboard**.

"Get off the train!" a squat man ordered. His round face and red cheeks did not match the

....

fortunate lucky
aboard on the train

sharpness of his voice.

"Get all your things out of the train! Take off your clothes. A doctor must examine you before you enter Poland."

Can you imagine? Taking off your clothes just like that in the middle of a train yard? Tovah, doctors examine you often because of your crooked back. Is this the way they treat you?

I fought them. I would not take off my clothes for them.

"Do as I say!" the guard **barked** at me. "Or you will be sent back, all of you."

From the fierceness of his voice I knew he **would not hesitate to turn us over** to the Russian police.

I could not have my family returned to Berdichev because of me. I took off my clothes.

I huddled beside Mama as we stood in our underwear in the waning daylight outside the boxcar. Aunt Rachel had made this underwear for me. It was white cotton and very pretty. She had made me two

....

sharpness mean sound
barked yelled
would not hesitate to turn us over would send us

sets, but one was stolen from me as I swam in the Teterev this past summer.

I thought of the things the Russians had taken from my family as I stood in the train yard and I was angry. Why, Tovah? Why is it that if a Russian peasant does not get what he wants, he **feels justified in stealing** it from a Jew?

Papa and the boys undressed on the opposite side of the car. At least they allowed us that much privacy.

Mama and I, we had folded our clothes on top of our bags in the dry grass along the track. The guards picked up our clothes and our belongings and took them away. Even my rucksack with Mama's candlesticks.

Before I could yell to them to bring our things back, the doctor came.

He growled at us. I could not understand his words, but he made it clear what he wanted. He ordered us to remove our underwear.

This doctor, he **stank of** vomit and schnapps.

....

feels justified in stealing thinks it is fair to steal
stank of smelled bad like

His breath choked my throat and I thought I would be sick. Mama did not seem to notice his **stench**. She smiled and nodded to him. Perhaps she feared he would send us back to Russia. Why else would she act so?

Mama helped me to remove my underwear, **shielding** my body with her own. Her gold locket hung between her breasts. "Keep quiet for once, Rifka," she whispered in my ear. "Stay behind me."

I covered my nakedness with my hands as best I could, but Mama, she acted as if stripping before the Polish doctor was no trouble, like we did this every day. She pretended this, I think, to protect me.

The doctor examined us. He took longer with Mama. I could hardly believe this brave woman was the same who wept with fear in your cellar last night. The doctor spent so much time with Mama, he hardly noticed me.

When he did turn his attention to me, the way he looked **gave me gooseflesh**. Tovah, you are so

....

stench bad smell
shielding hiding and protecting
gave me gooseflesh made me feel disgusted

practical. You will say I had gooseflesh because we stood naked outside in the cold, but it was not the cold that caused me to shiver.

The doctor made me feel dirty. He looked in my eyes and my mouth and my hair. "Are you sick?" he asked me in Russian.

I kept my eyes down. I **could not stand** to look at him. I stared instead at my toes curled tight in the stones at the edge of the tracks. I prayed the doctor would just go away.

He yelled at me, something in Polish. Mama spoke with him.

Then she took my hand and led me into a small building. In the building, a woman sprayed us with something **vile**. It burned my skin and my scalp, my nose and my eyes.

Finally the Polish guards allowed us back onto the train. They returned our clothes to us and our bags, **stinking of fumigation**. My eyes watered from the stench of it.

....

could not stand did not want

vile really bad

stinking of fumigation smelling like the chemicals sprayed on them to kill diseases

That was not the worst, though. When I lifted my rucksack, it was not as heavy as it had been before. I searched the entire bag, emptying it out on the floor of the train, but Mama's candlesticks were gone.

"So they stole our candlesticks," Mama said. "It could be worse, Rifka, much worse. Stop **sniffling** and finish getting dressed."

We pulled our clothes back on before Papa and Nathan and Saul joined us. Mama sighed with relief as they climbed into the car.

I turned away from their nakedness. How could the **Poles** do this to my papa, to my brothers? How could the Poles do this to me?

The train started moving before Papa and the boys finished dressing. That is how we entered Poland.

I have never been in another country before, not even in another village. You know how the Russians kept us, Tovah, like prisoners, never permitting us to travel. Russia has not been so bad for you. With money, Russia can be very good, even for a Jew. For us it was a prison.

....

sniffling crying
Poles people from Poland

Poland does not look that different from Berdichev. The same crooked cottages, the same patchy roads, the same bony fences leaning into the dust. Looking out from the train, we see people dressed like us, in browns and blacks; people wrapped in layers of clothes. The women bundle their heads in kerchiefs, the men shuffle along in ankle coats and boots. Will it be like this in America, too?

I will stop writing for now. My head **throbs** and my body aches from all that has happened.

Shalom, my cousin,
Rifka

....

throbs hurts

BEFORE YOU MOVE ON...

1. **Conclusions** Reread page 32. Why did the doctor examine the people?
2. **Character** What shows you that Rifka was angry about how she and her family were treated?

LOOK AHEAD Could things get worse in Poland? Read pages 35–41 to find out.

**Rifka gets sick with typhus. The rest of the family
also gets sick. Rifka and Saul are alone.**

Casual gift, oh, gift unutile,
Life, why wert thou given me?
Why should Fate thus grant us futile
Terms of doomed mortality? . . .
—Pushkin

October 5, 1919
Motziv, Poland

Dear Tovah,

I thought we would be in America by now, but we
remain in Poland, **stranded by illness**.

The sickness began with me. My legs and head
started aching shortly after we crossed the Polish
border.

---

stranded by illness forced to stay because we are sick

I told Papa, "I am tired. That spray has made me sick."

By the time we arrived in Motziv my head pounded and my body hurt as if the train had **run over me**. I wanted only to rest. The motion of the train **tormented me**. I begged Papa for us to stop.

Mama and Papa took me off the train in Motziv. I did not know Papa had a cousin here, did you, Tovah? Papa's cousin did not have room for us, but he **took us in** anyway.

I don't remember very well what happened the first few weeks in Motziv. We slept on the floor in the shed of my father's cousin. I had dreams, terrible dreams about the guards at the train station and **cossacks** and entire forests chasing after me. Such nightmares!

I could not move at all. I felt imprisoned under a mound of stones.

I remember Papa down on the floor beside me, putting a damp cloth on my head. Papa is so good at

....

run over me hit me
tormented me made me feel pain
took us in let us stay with him
cossacks soldiers from southern Russia

nursing, but each time he placed the cloth over my eyes, I felt the weight of it crushing my head to the floor.

I tried to pull away from him, but whenever I moved, the pain exploded inside me. I begged Papa to stop, but the words would not come out. I could hardly draw breath, there was such a heaviness on my chest.

Saul says a student of medicine came to examine me. Papa had found a student to come who spoke Russian. By then **a rash had crept under my armpits** and across my back and my stomach. I had a cough that threatened to split me in two each time it erupted from me.

I had typhus.

The medical student said, "Her infection started in Russia. Someone she had contact with there gave this to her."

I wanted to tell this skinny, **pock-faced** man that he was wrong, that my illness did not come from

....

nursing taking care of us

a rash had crept under my armpits my skin became red and bumpy under my arms

pock-faced acne-scarred

Russia. I knew where it started. It came from the doctor at the Polish border. I tried to explain this to the man, but I could not speak.

"You must say nothing about **the nature of her illness** to anyone," the medical student told Papa. "Not even to your cousin. As for the child, she will probably die. Most do. That's how it goes with typhus."

I remember very little, Tovah, but I do remember that. **Those words cut through the fever and the pain.** When I heard them, I wished I could die. If I died, I would be free of my suffering.

But if I died, I would never reach America.

I remember Mama crying. I tried to speak, to say I would not die, that nothing would **hold me back from** America, but she couldn't hear me. No one could hear me.

"I should send you all back to Russia," the medical student said. "But the child would never survive the trip."

....

the nature of her illness the type of sickness she has

Those words cut through the fever and the pain. I could hear what he said even though I was very sick.

hold me back from stop me from going to

Papa begged him to let us stay. "I promise to care for her," he said.

The medical student agreed.

I **lapsed into** sleep on the floor in the miserable little shed while the typhus **raged inside me**.

Meanwhile, Mama and Papa and Nathan grew sick. They developed the typhus too. Only Saul managed to stay healthy. Saul is too much of an ox to get sick, Tovah.

Three men took Mama and Papa and Nathan in a cart to a hospital at the other end of Motziv.

I wept to see them go. I was still so sick, but I wept to see them. As they carried Papa out and loaded him into the cart beside Mama, I thought my life was over.

"Take me too!" I cried, but I had improved compared to Mama and Papa and Nathan.

"Motziv is full of typhus," the cart driver said. "We need the beds for the dying."

They left me with Saul, of all people. Saul, who never has a kind word for me. Saul, who pulls my hair

....

lapsed into began to
raged inside me hurt my body

and punches me, even though Mama says at sixteen he should know better. Saul, with his big ears and his big feet, was all I had for a nurse.

It is **a wonder** I did not die from the typhus. When Saul remembered, he held water to my lips so I could drink.

In my dreams and when I woke, I **fretted over** Mama and Papa and Nathan. Were they already dead?

"Where is Mama?" I asked each time I woke from **a restless fever sleep**. "Where is Papa?"

Saul turned his face away. He could not stand the smell of me; I could tell by the way his mouth tightened. "Go back to sleep, Rifka," he said. He always said the same. "Go back to sleep."

Once I woke to find Saul kneeling beside me, holding my hands down. His dark hair curled wildly around his ears. "What are you doing to yourself?" he kept asking.

I had been dreaming about Mama's candlesticks. I was holding them against my chest. Hands, dozens of

....

a wonder very surprising

fretted over worried about

a restless fever sleep sleeping badly because of a fever hands, reached out of the darkness to take them from me. I **tore at** the hands, trying to get them off me, trying to get them off Mama's candlesticks.

"Look what you've done to yourself," Saul said, touching the **tail** of his shirt to my chest.

In my sleep, I had clawed at my chest until it bled.

Tovah, my hand is too weak to continue and **my eyes blur at** these tiny letters, but I will write again soon.

Shalom,
Rifka

....

tore at fought, attacked
tail end
my eyes blur at it is hard for me to see

BEFORE YOU MOVE ON...

1. **Cause and Effect** Why did Rifka's family have to stay in Poland?

2. **Inference** Reread page 38. Why did the medical student say the family should not tell anyone about the typhus?

LOOK AHEAD Read pages 42–51 to find out how Rifka and Saul help each other.

Rifka gets well again. Saul gets a job and rents a room for himself and Rifka. Rifka visits her mother in the hospital.

═══════════════════════════════════════

A thirst in spirit, through the gloom
Of an unpeopled waste I blundered . . .
—Pushkin

❧

November 3, 1919
Motziv, Poland

Dear Tovah,

I am doing much better now.

When I was well enough to move, Saul went out and found a new room for us to live in. "We cannot stay any longer in this shed," he said. Papa's family did not try to keep us from leaving. We had brought illness with us, and bad luck. We had taken from their table food they **could not spare**.

....

could not spare could not live without

The room Saul found for us is in a cheap, **run-down inn**. The innkeeper hosts a large market outside his establishment every Wednesday. **Merchants bring their wares** and the innkeeper sells tea and rolls and buns. I think he makes a lot of money.

Market days are noisy. When my head aches, I **cannot bear it**. On my good days, though, I like to look out at the **commotion**.

Saul says the innkeeper is a thief, but we will stay here until Mama and Papa and Nathan are out of the hospital.

Saul found work to pay for our room and our food. He sorts apples in an orchard outside the village. At dawn, before leaving for work, Saul goes out to the street. He brings back breakfast for us, a herring and two rolls.

Each morning, when he comes with the food, Tovah, he splits it exactly in half. Even though he is bigger and needs more, he divides our food evenly.

Each day, we eat our herring and roll in a few bites

....

run-down inn old, small hotel
Merchants bring their wares People sell things
cannot bear it suffer
commotion crowds

and lick our fingertips to catch the crumbs. Then Saul leaves.

One day I took only a bite of my herring and decided to save the rest.

I told Saul I was not hungry.

It was a lie. I was hungry. I am hungry all the time. When I am awake, all I think about is food. When I sleep, I dream of it. My stomach **twists and burns** with emptiness.

But on this morning I thought, for once Saul is nice to me. I should be the same with him. Saul is working, he needs to eat more than I do. If I save my share of breakfast, it will be waiting for him in the evening when he returns.

I was still weak, but I knew I must get up and **stow** the herring and roll in the closet near my **cot**. If I did not put it away from myself, I would eat it.

My stomach knotted painfully, and **in spite of my best intentions** I took another bite of the herring

....

twists and burns hurts, aches

stow hide

cot bed

in spite of my best intentions even though I wanted to be nice and save the food for Saul before I closed the closet door. I hope you will not think I am too selfish, Tovah.

I **turned my back on** my precious food and tumbled into my cot, falling asleep immediately.

Movement in the room awakened me.

At first I thought Saul had come back, but it was not Saul. It was the girl whose father owns the inn. She sat on the edge of my cot, her thick, greasy braid hanging down her back.

She was eating something, herring and roll. The closet door was open. She was eating my herring and roll!

"Thief!" I cried in Russian. "Give me back my food!"

She ignored me. She sat on my cot, chewing.

I tried to get my roll back from her. She **brushed me aside** and laughed at me, Tovah.

She has so much food of her own. Always, when I see her passing by my room, she is chewing, her red cheeks **swollen like a squirrel with a nut**. The girl

---

turned my back on ignored
brushed me aside ignored me
swollen like a squirrel with a nut filled with food

had spied on me. She had seen me save my food in the little closet and had come in and taken it for herself.

That family, they have rolls and buns all the time. It is the father's business. I drag myself from the drafty room Saul and I share and stand, **swaying unsteadily** in front of the bakery cases, staring at the innkeeper's food. I am so hungry, but no one **offers me a crumb**. The girl will be chewing, her tongue flicking out to catch a piece of bun and bring it back into her mouth again. She has all this food and she has to steal from me.

When Saul got back that evening, I told him about the girl stealing my food. I thought he would catch her and beat her up. Saul said, "Next time don't save your food, Rifka. Eat it. Then she can't take it from you."

And that was that.

With Saul gone all day, I felt lonely. Not that **he was such good company**, but I hated being alone,

---

swaying unsteadily almost falling

offers me a crumb gives me any food at all

he was such good company I liked being with him very much separated from Mama and Papa. In Berdichev, I could have gone to you, or to Aunt Anna, or to Bubbe Ruth.

But I was in a strange country, with no one to go to. I certainly would not go to the innkeeper's daughter, that dirty thief.

So when I grew strong enough, I started walking around Motziv. I found my way to the low, **sprawling** hospital where they were keeping Mama. I discovered a wooden ledge outside the window of Mama's ward and climbed on it to look in on her.

Mama lay in a narrow bed, as white as the sheet on top of her. Everything about Mama was white except her black hair. Her hair was like a dark **stain** on the hospital **linens** and her eyes remained closed, her thick lashes resting on white cheeks. She looked dead, Tovah, and I kept staring, waiting for her to move.

When the hospital workers caught me looking in at Mama, they yelled at me. They chased me away from the building. They couldn't understand that I

....

sprawling large
stain spot
linens sheets

needed to see Mama move. I needed to know she was alive. So the next day I came back, and the next day, and the next.

The Polish language has started making sense to me, Tovah. I didn't need to be clever to know I should stay out of the hospital workers' way, but I could not stay away from Mama.

Then, just this morning, a doctor caught me looking in at Mama. He did not chase me away. He lifted me down off the ledge.

"What are you doing here?" the doctor asked.

"I am watching over my mama," I explained.

The doctor asked, "Have you had the typhus?"

"Yes," I told him. "But I am better now."

The doctor said, "Come." He led me inside the hospital and sat me in a chair next to Mama's cot. "Once you have suffered through the typhus, you cannot have it again," the doctor explained. "It will **do you no harm** to sit with her. It may do her some

....

The Polish language has started making sense to me
I have started to understand Polish

do you no harm not hurt you

good." I held Mama's hand and talked to her all the rest of today.

I even got to eat a potato out of the big pot brought by a lady who feeds the hospital patients.

They were good potatoes, Tovah. Since I have been sick, everything tastes good. How skinny I've become. But not Saul; he is as big as a horse. His legs have grown so long just since we left Russia. You should see **how they sprout from his pants**.

Even with all my things on, my underwear and my two extra dresses, and my cloak and shawl, I still do not look fat. Remember how in Berdichev the Russian guards would come to inspect the homes of the Jews? They made certain we owned no more than **our allowance**. Always, when the guards were coming, Mama would say, "Rifka, put all your clothes on." I would rush and throw my dresses over my head and stand out in front of the house to watch.

The guards would search through our rooms.

....

how they sprout from his pants how much longer his legs are than his pants

our allowance what they let us have

They did not find more than two of anything. How could they find anything extra in our house? In your house there are many **fine** things, Tovah, but they never inspected your house.

The guards would look at me, layered in all my belongings, and say, "Hmmm, fat kid." With my dresses and my **cloak and my shawl** piled on top of me, I looked as short and round as a barrel.

I am no longer round, but I am still short. I wonder if I will ever grow, Tovah. Maybe it will be all right that I am short in America. If I could get Bubbe Ruth to come, there would at least be two of us.

If I could get Bubbe Ruth to come. She does not stay because she is comfortable and safe like you and Hannah and Uncle Avrum. Bubbe Ruth stays because she is afraid to leave, afraid for things to change. I am afraid too, but not so afraid that I want to come back.

I would like it best if you and Hannah and Uncle Avrum and Aunt Anna and Bubbe Ruth and all the

....

fine expensive
cloak and my shawl coat and my scarf

others were coming to America, too. I am trying to be clever, Tovah, but how much more clever I could be **surrounded by my family**.

Shalom, my cousin,
Rifka

....

surrounded by my family with my family near me

BEFORE YOU MOVE ON...

1. **Character's Motive** Rifka saved her food for Saul. Why? Reread pages 43–44.

2. **Flashback** Reread pages 49–50. Rifka remembers her life in Berdichev. What was her life like there?

LOOK AHEAD Read pages 52–62 to find out who Rifka meets on the train ride to Warsaw.

The family survives typhus, so they continue on their journey. Rifka meets a Polish girl who is sick. Rifka combs the girl's hair.

===

> *. . . In hope, in torment, we are turning*
> *Toward freedom, waiting her command . . .*
> —Pushkin

28

November 27, 1919
en route to Warsaw

Dear Tovah,

Many of the typhus patients at the hospital in Motziv died. We all survived. Now, **at last, we are on our way** to Warsaw. All of us—me, Mama, Papa, Nathan, and Saul.

Warsaw is where we **pick up** the money for our

....

en route going, traveling
at last, we are on our way after a long time, we are going
pick up get

steamship tickets. My older brothers, Isaac and Reuben and Asher, have worked hard to save the money so we could join them in America. These other brothers of mine, they left Russia fourteen years ago, before my birth. Do *you* even remember them, Tovah?

They are my brothers, my family, but I don't know them. Papa showed me their letters. In my mind the letters came from strangers living in a distant land.

Then, only the day before we **fled** from Russia, the Red Cross posted the message on the board. Isaac and Reuben and Asher, they were sending for us. Remember how I ran to tell you our news? I wonder, Tovah, if the message still hangs there in the center of the village.

I am certain Warsaw is a wonderful city. When people in Motziv say the word "Warsaw," their voices deepen and they give a little kick on the end, like this: "Warsaw-ha!" It reminds me of the way we do in Berdichev when we speak of America.

Our train passes small herds of cattle grazing on yellowed grass and I remember the cows of Berdichev.

....

fled escaped

The peasant girls drove them along the road past our house every night at sunset. Those cows were not bony as these are. I loved sitting on the front step watching the fat brown **beasts lumber past.** **The earth shivered beneath their clopping weight as the sun set in a ball of fire.** Those girls sang in such beautiful harmony.

When I read your Pushkin, I remember those cows, and the girls' singing.

Poland is so cold and flat and colorless. Only pine trees, scrubby, wretched pine trees, sweep past the window of the train. Maybe in the spring it is better, maybe there are flowers. Maybe the sky is something other than gray. Now, it is nearly December, and I shiver at the cold of Poland.

It is odd to see Mama and Papa and Nathan so changed. In Berdichev, Mama kept us all well **on practically nothing.** You know what a baker she is. Always the smell of yeast clung to her.

----

beasts lumber past cows walk by slowly

The earth shivered beneath their clopping weight as the sun set in a ball of fire. Their steps shook the ground as the bright sun set.

on practically nothing without much food

Many times she would send me to your house with a basket of pastries or a cake, or her thick dark bread. There is no baking for her now.

Papa's dark eyes have lost their spark since the typhus, and Mama's long black hair does not shine as it once did. Even Nathan, with his thick black curls and his strong dimpled jaw, has hollowed cheeks and circles beneath his eyes. I cannot tell how I look, but Mama sometimes strokes my cheek and sighs. Her fingers are bony and rough.

Only Saul still glows with health from his clumsy feet to his big red ears.

I must tell you of this noisy, crowded, stinking train we are riding north out of Motziv. The freight train from Berdichev was more comfortable. Here people push against one another on every bench. The cars are **drafty and reek of old bedding**. Between the chugging and the clacking tracks and the endless Polish **babble**, the noise never stops pressing against you. Worse still, there is no place **to relieve yourself**

....

drafty and reek of old bedding windy and smell like old bed sheets

babble talking

to relieve yourself to go to the bathroom

and I drank two cups of tea before we boarded. I could not sit still a moment longer.

"I am going for a walk," I told Mama.

Mama nodded, still chewing slowly her lunch of cold potato and roll. I had finished the last bite of mine long ago.

At the back of our car a peasant girl sat on a bench with a baby sucking at her breast. At first I thought the girl was older, but when she looked up, I saw she was your age, Tovah, near sixteen.

Her blond hair hung thinly down from her kerchief, tickling the baby's bald head. The baby's fingers played on the girl's cheek as it nursed.

The girl noticed me staring. "You like babies?" she asked in Polish, talking over the heads of the passengers beside her.

I nodded and **fiddled with** the knot of my kerchief.

"You have beautiful hair," she said. "Mine . . . " She took her free hand and **flipped the wisps** of hair over her shoulder. "My sister used to **fix** my hair.

....

fiddled with nervously played with
flipped the wisps moved the pieces
fix brush and style

56

Until she married and moved away. I am going to visit her now, my sister."

I do not know what made me offer. Maybe it was the sweetness of the baby, maybe the friendliness of the girl. "I used to fix my cousin's hair," I said in Polish. "I could fix yours so you will look nice for your sister . . . if you'd like."

She was happy to let me fix her hair. I pushed into the narrow space between the bench and the back of the train car and removed her kerchief.

Her head stank. Strands of hair clustered in oily clumps. Most terrible, though, were big round sores all over her **scalp**.

My fingers hesitated. I did not wish to touch the girl's head, yet neither did I wish to insult her. I gathered the ends of her hair and began unknotting the tangles.

Tilting her head back, the girl sighed as I worked my fingers through the snarls.

The baby pulled its mouth off the girl's breast

....

scalp skin under her hair

My fingers hesitated. I stopped before I touched her hair.

and looked up at me. Its mouth opened into a milky smile.

"You have a nice baby," I said.

The girl turned and looked me over. "You are not Polish."

I was afraid everyone on the train heard her. I worried they'd send me back to Berdichev as the Polish border guards had threatened, or that they'd chase me away as the nurses did in Motziv. **To my relief,** the other passengers ignored us and the girl turned back around.

"I am from Ukraine," I whispered. "I am going with my family to America."

"America!" the girl said. "America."

The man sitting beside her **inched away**, forcing an old woman on the end of the bench to **plant her feet firmly** on the floor to keep from falling.

"America," the girl repeated. "What will you do there?"

I was silent for a little time.

....

To my relief, I was glad that
inched away moved away from her slowly
plant her feet firmly put her feet

"I will do everything there," I answered.

The girl **threw back her head** and laughed. Standing over her, I saw that several of her teeth were missing.

She said, "Why would you want to go to America? You can do everything you want right here. I would never leave Poland."

"Never?" I asked.

"I can't imagine going out my door and finding anything else. Look at it out there. That is home."

I looked out the train window. There was a boy running across a frozen field with a black dog loping along at his side. For a moment I saw Poland as she saw it.

Then my eyes saw the **bleakness** outside the window again and I **felt a chill creep down my spine**.

"There," I said, smoothing out the last tangle from her hair and backing away shyly. "I must return to my family."

She put a finger to her lips, revealing a cracked

....

threw back her head moved her head back
bleakness ugliness
felt a chill creep down my spine got cold

and reddened nail. Her baby slept with its little nose squashed against her breast.

"Good luck to you in America," she whispered.

I **stumbled** back up the aisle of the **lurching** train, thrown against this one's shoulder, squeezing past that one. The smell of cheese filled the car. **My mouth watered at the stench of it.**

I slid back into my place between Mama and Nathan and looked around at the other people in the car, listening to their conversations.

I felt your Pushkin inside my rucksack and I wanted to get it out and write my thoughts. I am filling the pages of our book quickly, Tovah, even with my writing so small and fine.

"Mama?" I asked, feeling her elbow rub against my ribs with the motion of the train. "Can I get off for a little while at the next station? The stops are so long. Could I get off just for a moment?"

"No."

"But Mama, I have to go . . . "

---

stumbled walked slowly

lurching jerking

My mouth watered at the stench of it. It made me hungry.

"No," Mama said. "I told you not to drink that tea this morning."

"I'm bored, Mama," I said.

I was afraid to tell her the truth, Tovah. To tell her I wanted only to find a quiet corner, where I could open our Pushkin. She did not like your teaching me Pushkin in Berdichev. **If Mama had her way**, I would know how to cook, and sew, and **keep the Sabbath**. That is all.

"You are bored?" Mama said. "So I'll hire you a band. You are not getting off this train, Rifka. What if it left without you? **You want we should** get separated? You want to spend the rest of your life in Poland? No, Rifka, you stay right where you are. Here I can **keep an eye on you**. Here you are safe."

So I kept my thoughts in my head until this moment. Mama and Saul snore softly at the end of the bench. Papa and Nathan have gone off to stretch their long legs.

As I write, I am thinking that sometimes I don't

If Mama had her way If I did what Mama wanted

keep the Sabbath rest and pray every Friday night to Saturday night

You want we should Do you want us to

keep an eye on you watch you

like growing up, Tovah. Sometimes I wish I could run back to Berdichev, into Bubbe Ruth's arms, and **lose myself inside her warmth**. She protected me from everything around me and inside me.

But then at other times I am so glad to be who I am. Rifka Nebrot. Only daughter and youngest child of Ethel and Beryl Nebrot. Baby sister of Isaac and Asher and Reuben and Nathan and Saul. Traveling forward—to America.

When I think of myself that way, even though we are homeless and our lives are in danger even now, still I believe everything will turn out well.

Shalom, my cousin,
Rifka

....

lose myself in her warmth be comforted by her

BEFORE YOU MOVE ON...

1. **Comparisons** Reread pages 58–59. Compare how Rifka and the Polish girl she met felt about going to America.

2. **Character's Motive** Reread pages 60–61. Why did Rifka ask her mother if she could get off the train?

LOOK AHEAD Read pages 63–70 to find out if Rifka can get a ticket to America.

***Rifka is sick. The doctors will not let her leave
for America. Her parents try to find a way
to keep the family together.***

. . . Goal, there can be none before me,
Empty-hearted, idle-willed.
Life's monotony rolls o'er me,
Tired with longings unfulfilled.
—Pushkin

❧

November 30, 1919
Warsaw, Poland

Dear Tovah,

What should I do? I **hold the worst news in my
heart**. Whatever shall I do?

As soon as we finished **our business** at the bank
in Warsaw, we followed directions to the steamship

....

hold the worst news in my heart have just heard very
bad news

our business doing what we needed to do

office. How rich we felt with all the money my brothers had sent us from America. How **eager** we were to start our journey across the ocean.

Before they sell you your ticket, though, Tovah, you must have an examination by a doctor.

I think doctors are the cruelest men upon this earth. This doctor, who worked for the steamship company, took me and Mama into a room. He examined us for deformities and disease.

He examined our bodies and our eyes.

"Take off your kerchiefs," he said. "I will check your scalps."

My head had been itching terribly for the past day. I gladly removed my kerchief and gave my head a good scratching.

The doctor washed his hands after he examined me.

"Mrs. Nebrot," he told my mother, "you have passed your examination. You may go now to buy your ticket."

....

eager excited and ready

"Come along, Rifka," Mama said, **gathering her belongings**.

"No," the doctor said. "I am sorry. Your daughter cannot join you. Our company will not sell her **passage** to America."

Mama said, "You don't understand. She must go to America."

"She can't," the doctor answered. "She has a skin disease, ringworm. You see these sores on her scalp?" I thought of the Polish girl on the train, the girl with the baby. She had sores on her scalp.

Mama's dark eyes widened. "Rifka, Rifka," she murmured. Her hands shook. "How do we get rid of this—this ringworm?"

"There is a treatment," the doctor said. "But it takes many months."

All of me went numb. Only my heart beat **thickly** in my chest.

Before he showed us out of his room, the doctor wrote something on a piece of paper. He handed it to

....

gathering her belongings taking her things

passage a ticket on a boat

All of me went numb. I was so upset I could not feel anything.

thickly strongly

Mama and told her to give the paper to the man at the steamship office window.

Papa tried **bribing** the steamship officials. It is a trick he learned in Berdichev from your father, a trick where **money put in the right pocket** can get you almost anything.

"Here," Papa said to the man in the steamship office, pushing our precious money into his hand. "Please, take this to make my daughter Rifka a ticket."

The man looked at Papa's money. He looked at the five of us standing before him. "Wait here," he said.

He went to the other room, the room where the doctor sat. He came back shortly.

"I'm sorry," he said, returning to his post at the window.

"Is it not enough?" Papa asked, reaching into his pockets. "You need to have more?"

"No more," the man said. "What you ask is impossible. The child cannot go."

....

bribing giving money to

money put in the right pocket giving money to people who can help you

"Why can't I go?" I demanded.

The man **paid no attention** to me. He spoke to Mama and Papa. "If the child arrives in America with this disease, the Americans will turn her around and send her right back to Poland. My company will have to pay the cost of her return. If my company has to do this for your daughter, the doctor and I will no longer have our jobs. I'm sorry. There's nothing I can do."

Tovah! I can't go to America! They will let Mama and Papa and Saul and Nathan go. But they won't let me. I cannot stay here in Warsaw without Mama and Papa! How can I live without Mama and Papa to care for me, to protect me?

Yesterday Mama gave me a handful of money and sent me outside to wait for her and Papa.

"You stay out of trouble," Mama said. "We'll try our luck at *this* steamship company; perhaps they will not mind about your ringworm."

Outside, a bony old man with a nose like a **parsnip** sat with a basket at his feet full of round

---

paid no attention did not listen
parsnip long vegetable

orange fruit. I stared at him and stared at him. Finally I went over.

"What is this?" I asked in Polish, pointing to the fruit. From a distance, I had seen a similar fruit in Motziv at the market outside our inn. That fruit was small, more yellow than orange, with patches of green. These were perfect **autumn-colored** balls.

"Oranges," the old man answered. He had no teeth in his mouth.

"How much for one?" I asked, **inhaling** the bright smell of fruit wafting up from his basket. **My stomach grumbled eagerly and my mouth grew wet.**

"How much you have?" he asked. When he spoke, bits of spittle stretched between his lips. He stared straight at me. I was not being clever then, Tovah. I held out my handful of money. He took it all and handed me one orange.

A few moments later, Mama came out and saw me biting through the bitter skin of the fruit. "Where did you get that?" she asked. "Where is the money I gave

....

autumn-colored orange

inhaling breathing in

My stomach grumbled eagerly and my mouth grew wet. I felt hunger in my stomach and mouth.

you, Rifka?"

I took her to the old man, but the man cried, "There you are! Thief! You steal my oranges! Help! Police! What monster are you, to steal from an old man!"

"I did not!" I cried. "I paid you. You took all the money I had!"

"Liar!" the old man screamed. "Liar and thief!" His spittle flew through the air. A drop landed on the back of my hand. I rubbed and rubbed it against my coat but I could not **get the feel of it off me**. Finally Papa gave him more money to quiet him.

I lost our food money, Tovah. Mama yelled at me and Saul made a horrible face. I bit my lip to keep from crying. The taste of the orange still danced in my mouth. I will never eat another orange as long as I live!

Mama said, "What will we do? We have to eat." "Hush," Papa said. "I will think of something."

"It is not your fault, Rifka," Nathan whispered. He tried smiling, but **his dimples barely showed**.

....

get the feel of it off me forget that his spit touched me
his dimples barely showed he did not look like he was really happy

Now we have no money for food. Tovah, I think there is no hope I will ever be clever.

That tells you about Warsaw. How can Mama and Papa leave me in such a city?

Warsaw is bigger than any city I have ever seen. The buildings are so tall, I get dizzy looking up at them. There are carriages that move without horses to pull them. They are called "cars," and **they prowl the streets like frenzied wolves**.

Warsaw is a horrible place, Tovah. I can never stay here.

Pray for me, please,
Rifka

....

they prowl the streets like frenzied wolves they move very fast

BEFORE YOU MOVE ON...

1. **Conflict** Why did the doctor say Rifka could not have a steamship ticket?

2. **Conclusions** Reread pages 68–70. Why did Rifka think Warsaw was a very bad place?

LOOK AHEAD Will Rifka stay in Europe without her family? Read pages 71–75 to find out.

Rifka and her parents meet with a person who helps Jewish immigrants. The family has to make a hard decision.

═══════════════════════════════════════

. . . As conquered by the last cold air,
When winter whistles in the wind,
Alone upon a branch that's bare
A trembling leaf is left behind.
—Pushkin

ಌ

December 1, 1919
Warsaw, Poland

Dear Tovah,

Papa and Mama met with a lady from the HIAS. That is the Hebrew Immigrant Aid Society. They are a group of people who help Jews with troubles like ours. The lady said the HIAS has workers all over the world. I wonder why we never met any in Berdichev or Motziv. Have you heard of them?

The lady from the HIAS gave us money to buy food. She sat with us in our room and listened to our troubles. She was no taller than I am. **Wisps** of silver hair kept **escaping** from **a bun** on the top of her bead.

She said, "Mr. and Mrs. Nebrot, you and your two sons should leave for America as planned. But, Rifka must stay until her ringworm heals."

"To leave a child of twelve?" Papa said. "How can we do such a thing?"

"It is not so unusual," the HIAS lady said. "We have handled many such cases."

Awful things are happening to me, Tovah. My hair is falling out, my long blond hair. I have a bald patch over one ear and another on the back of my head. I can cover it with the kerchief, but it itches and itches. I know I must be ugly because Mama's eyes look away from me all the time now.

"Can't Mama stay with me?" I asked.

The lady from the HIAS said, "If your mama goes to America, she can work and make money for the family. She can make a home for your father and your brothers. If your mama stays in Europe with you, she

---

Wisps Thin strings
escaping falling down
a bun the bunch of hair

will cost the family money. Only you must stay, Rifka."

"I will not stay in Warsaw," I told the lady from the HIAS. "If my family leaves me in Warsaw, I will find a way back to my home in Berdichev."

The lady from the HIAS said, "I want you to leave Warsaw also, but not for Berdichev. **The cure for your illness awaits you** in Belgium."

Mama said, "Belgium? What is Belgium? I have never heard of this place."

"It is the best place for Rifka now," the HIAS lady said. "The people of Belgium **open their arms and their homes to** immigrants."

That is what I am, Tovah. That is what you are when you are wandering between two worlds. You are an immigrant.

The HIAS lady said, "We can arrange for Rifka to stay with a family in Antwerp. She will go each day to a hospital and get treatment for her ringworm. When you are all better, Rifka, you can sail to America right from Antwerp and join your mama and papa and all your brothers."

The cure for your illness awaits you You will find the cure for the ringworm

open their arms and their homes to welcome

"I don't want to stay with a family I don't know," I said. I remembered the innkeeper's daughter in Motziv, the one who ate my herring. What if the family I stay with in Belgium is like hers?

I do not want to be anywhere without my family. Even Saul would be better than no one. If they would just let Saul stay with me.

Saul does not want to stay. All Saul cares about is getting to America.

The HIAS lady said, "In Antwerp there will be someone from my organization **to look out for you, to monitor your care**."

I said, "If I can't go to America, please send me back to Berdichev."

Papa said, "Rifka, the Russians are angry at our family in Berdichev. We have **cheated them of five strong boys**. The army wanted your brothers, they wanted Isaac and Asher and Reuben and Nathan and Saul. I could not let them have my sons."

Nathan sat with his hands clasped in his lap. Saul stood with his back to me, staring out the little

---

to look out for you, to monitor your care to protect you, to heal the disease

cheated them of five strong boys taken five strong boys from them window of our room.

"Rifka," Papa said, "you cannot go back to our home in Berdichev. We have no more home in Berdichev. You, too, would meet your death if you returned now. Your coming back would put all the family remaining, Tovah and Bubbe Ruth and Aunt Anna and all the others, in greater danger."

I don't want to put you in danger, Tovah. I must go to Belgium, I see that, but I feel so frightened. What will become of me?

Tovah, I am **like an orphan** now.

Shalom,
Rifka

....

like an orphan alone

BEFORE YOU MOVE ON...

1. **Paraphrase** Reread pages 72–75. Tell why Rifka had to go to Belgium and why her mother could not stay with her.

2. **Cause and Effect** Reread page 75. What would happen if Rifka returned to Berdichev?

LOOK AHEAD Read pages 76–89 to find out about Rifka's new home.

Rifka celebrates her thirteenth birthday alone in Belgium. She loses her hair. A kind woman named Sister Katrina tries to cure her ringworm.

<hr>

. . . Sleep evades me, there's no light:
Darkness wraps the earth with slumber,
Only weary tickings number
The slow hours of the night. . . .
—Pushkin

ಶಿ

February 25, 1920
Antwerp, Belgium

Dear Tovah,

Saying good-bye to Mama and Papa hurt in my chest the way it hurt when Saul held me underwater too long. The night before, Mama had **slipped off** her gold locket. I had never seen Mama without

....

slipped off removed

her locket. It came from Papa, his wedding gift to her. Mama hung the gold chain around my neck. I **wrapped my hand around it** and felt Mama's warmth in the etched metal.

Papa gave me his tallis, his precious prayer shawl. He said a prayer over it first, kissed the **fringe**, then handed it to me.

"Why should she have Papa's tallis?" Saul muttered, "She is only a girl."

"Hush, Saul," Nathan said. "Don't make things worse."

The HIAS lady in Warsaw put me on my train the same day Mama, Papa, Nathan, and Saul left. I waved good-bye to them until my arm ached, but too soon, crowds pushed between us, and they were gone.

My train took me through Germany and into Belgium. So now I am in Antwerp. It has taken me a little while to **get settled**. The first room the Hebrew Immigrant Aid Society found for me was dark and stuffy, like the inside of your **wardrobe**, Tovah. Now I

....

wrapped my hand around it held it in my hand
fringe edge
get settled feel comfortable
wardrobe closet

am in a very nice room.

The couple who own this house are older even than Mama and Papa. They tell me to call them Gaston and Marie. Can you imagine, Tovah? They have very nice things. A quilt of blue squares covers my bed and a little red desk sits under the window. I sit at the desk for hours, fitting perfectly because I am so short, and I look out the window at the park below or read our Pushkin. I have a pitcher and bowl decorated with tiny blue flowers and a chest to keep my clothes in.

There is a painting on the wall over my bed. It shows a countryside covered with wildflowers. When I look at it, I think this is what it is like in America.

I have a braided rug to warm my feet. The woman, Marie, made it herself. She has made many of the things here.

This is the nicest place I have ever lived. My room is almost as **fine** as the rooms in your house, Tovah.

But it is not home. It can never be home without

....

fine nice, comfortable

Mama and Papa. I miss them so much.

Papa wrote that they have settled in New York City. His letters tell about their trip across the ocean and their apartment. They have water right outside their door and a real indoor toilet just down the hall. It is odd to think of Mama and Papa **living in such luxury**.

My thirteenth birthday came last week. I did not tell Marie and Gaston.

I had hoped to celebrate this birthday in America.

I remember my ninth birthday when you and Hannah gave me the doll. What a beautiful doll she was, with a china head. Every morning I would smear her face with herring, pretending she was eating breakfast, too.

Mama and Saul took that doll. I remember how they took her, along with the dress Aunt Rachel had made for me. I could never tell you this. Papa **forbade us to** speak to anyone about such matters. But Mama and Saul took my doll and my dress and traded them

....

living in such luxury having a nice home and nice things
forbade us to told us not to

at the market for potatoes. I swore I would not eat those potatoes, but I got hungry and I ate.

In America, no one will take my gifts from me.

So I am thirteen now. For Nathan and Saul's thirteenth birthdays, Mama and Papa **did a mitzvah**. I am just a girl. Still, girl or not, I think God would want me to do a mitzvah, too.

Early on the morning of my birthday, I crept down the stairs and took broken straws from the kitchen broom.

Back in my room, I wove the straws into a **Star of David**, a fragile golden Star of David. It took patience and time to twine the straws so they would hold together. When I finished, I set my star on the red desk beside Mama's locket and the sunlight fell on them both. I stood before the window, wrapped in Papa's tallis, and recited all the Hebrew prayers I held in my memory. Maybe you would think me foolish, Tovah, but I did a mitzvah. I celebrated my becoming a woman, just like the boys do when they become men.

---

did a mitzvah had a ceremony to celebrate becoming an adult
Star of David Jewish symbol

Later, I placed my Star of David between the pages of our Pushkin, so I could keep it forever to remember this day.

Before I went to sleep that night, I read over my letters to you. I **ran out of blank pages** in the book a long time ago. Now I write in the margins around the poetry. Someday I will get these letters to you, Tovah. I promise. When I reach America, Papa will show me how to send this properly and you will have your Pushkin back again. In America, I can buy my own Pushkin . . . and any other book I wish to read.

My hair is gone. All gone. I am as bald as the rabbi of Berdichev. I cover my **baldness** with a kerchief, but still I look very ugly.

I don't ever leave my room. It is winter. Back in our village, I was always first out to skate on the pond. In Antwerp, I do not go outside, except for my treatments.

The treatments are not so bad as I feared. I walk to the convent once a day. The nun in charge of my case

....

ran out of blank pages wrote on all of the empty pages
baldness bald head

is Sister Katrina. She washes my scalp with a green soap that makes my eyes water. Then she puts me under a violet light. The light warms my head.

"You don't mind the treatments, do you, Rifka?" Sister Katrina asks.

I smile and shake my head. I do not mind. In Belgium, where I am neither held nor loved, it feels good when Sister Katrina touches me, even if she does so only to **treat my ringworm.**

When my scalp is **perfectly** dry, Sister Katrina sprinkles it with powder. She gave me two new kerchiefs, pretty ones. She boils and dries them each time before I can wear them.

"Cleanliness is important in curing your disease," Sister Katrina says.

She also makes me clean my nails. "You can make the disease worse by scratching the sores with your fingers," she says.

I tell her, "My nails are clean. See!"

She says, "You can't see the germs that make the

....

treat my ringworm try to stop the disease
perfectly completely

ringworm, Rifka. Here, **scrub** your nails."

So I do.

I don't scratch my head that much anyway. Just sometimes I can't help it. Sister Katrina is teaching me Flemish. She taught me a prayer to say in my head when I need to scratch. I think saying the prayer is supposed to **keep my mind off** the itching. I am not sure it is right, though, for a Jew to say Catholic prayers. I say a Hebrew prayer instead.

The sister is nice. She has dimples even deeper than Nathan's: so deep, I can see them even when she is not smiling. Papa sends me money in his letters. He writes that I must pay Sister Katrina for the care she gives me.

I count out the money they send. I think Mama and Papa must be getting rich in America, working in the clothing factory. I think soon they will be as rich as Uncle Avrum.

Then I worry that maybe they are going without food to send this money to me.

....

scrub clean

keep my mind off make me think of something other than

Sister Katrina **accepts nothing**. "Keep it," she says. "You need it more."

She talks with me during my treatment. At first we spoke only in Polish, but I am **picking up** Flemish quickly.

After my treatments she makes tea. Sister Katrina tells me I am clever because I learn Flemish so easily. I thought you would like that, Tovah, that someone thinks I am clever.

"Really it is not so clever," I tell her. "It is nothing special. I just learn these things."

"You will learn even faster if you get out of your room," Sister Katrina says. "Antwerp is a lovely city. Go out, enjoy yourself."

"I like my room," I say. "It too is lovely. I am happy to stay there." I can't explain to her how I fear this city filled with strangers.

"You do not get enough exercise," Sister Katrina says. "You go from your room to the **convent** and back again. Explore more. Go on. It won't hurt you.

....

accepts nothing will not take the money
picking up learning
convent nuns' house for treatment

What you need, Rifka, is some fresh Belgian air."

It is not exercise and fresh air I need. It is Mama and Papa. How can I enjoy myself without Mama, without my family? I do not need exercise. All I need is to get better and to go to America.

Walking to and from the convent, I pass many beautiful sights. There are gardens everywhere, and even in the winter I can see how fine they are. I pass a market filled with fruits and vegetables and buckets of flowers of every color. And smells that make my stomach always eager to eat.

Right now I am sitting at the little desk in my room, looking out over the park. There are children who come every day. I'm beginning to recognize them. There is one girl, **built so much like Hannah**, slender with dark eyes and dark hair. Once or twice I have almost gone out only to be near her.

I would like to play with her, to play with all of them, but what if it is like Russia and they hate me because I am a Jew? What if it is like Poland and they

---

built so much like Hannah who looks a lot like Hannah

hate me because I am not a Pole? What if they hate me because I have no hair?

I wish I could be back with you, Tovah, and with Hannah. Remember how Hannah would dress me up and **coil my hair around** her fingers? When I grew sleepy, she would set me on the warm shelf of the tiled stove and cover me in furs and sing to me.

And you. You would talk, always talk.

"Listen to this, Rifka," you would say, and you would read me something from one of Uncle Avrum's big books. Or you would open the Pushkin and sometimes your voice would **go deep and husky**. I could not understand why, but tears would stand in both our eyes. Tovah, I loved the words that **sprang from your lips**. It is you, my cousin, who made me want to learn.

Hannah is like a fairy princess, so delicate and beautiful and sweet. You, Tovah, are like an old rabbi, clever and funny and brave.

Is Hannah still taking piano lessons? Marie plays

....

coil my hair around touch my hair with
go deep and husky sound deep and sleepy
sprang from your lips came out of your mouth

piano. She is playing now.

Don't tell this to Hannah, but I used to hate listening to her lessons. The teacher would scream and tears would roll down Hannah's cheeks. She never **got the notes right**.

It is you who can really play, Tovah, **and never a lesson of your own**. It amazed me how you could watch Hannah's lesson and then sit down after and play the music yourself. I never understood why Uncle Avrum didn't give you lessons.

When I asked Mama, she said, "Uncle Avrum won't give Tovah piano lessons because of her back."

"Well," I told Mama, "just because Tovah's back isn't straight doesn't mean she can't play the piano. When she was a baby and fell from the table did she hurt anything else? Did she hurt her hands so she couldn't play? No! So why can't Tovah have piano lessons?"

Mama said, "You couldn't understand, Rifka."

"I can," I insisted. "Explain to me."

....

got the notes right played well

and never a lesson of your own even though you never took any lessons

Mama said, "Uncle Avrum gives Hannah piano lessons so she can **catch** a good husband."

"What about Tovah?" I asked. "Doesn't Uncle Avrum want her to catch a good husband, too?"

Mama said, "Some girls **aren't meant to** marry, Rifka."

"But Tovah is smart and funny!" I cried. "And so clever . . . " I thought everyone **saw** you as I did.

Now that I am bald, I wonder. Maybe Mama would think I am one of those girls, too. One of those girls not meant to marry.

Sister Katrina says my hair will grow back. What if it doesn't? I think you would still love me, just as I love you. Bubbe Ruth, my dear little grandmother, she would love me, even with a bald head. But you are both very far away.

My own mama watched with such **sorrow** my hair falling out, and she left before it was done. What would she think if she saw me now? I have started

---

catch marry
aren't meant to will never
saw thought about
sorrow sadness

praying for my hair to grow back. Sometimes I even say Sister Katrina's prayer, even if it is for Catholics. I hope that does not make things worse for me.

Shalom, dear Tovah,
Rifka

BEFORE YOU MOVE ON...

1. **Character** Rifka loved her new home but said it could never be home without her mama and papa. What did this show about Rifka?

2. **Conclusions** Reread pages 85–86. Why was Rifka afraid to play with the children in the park?

LOOK AHEAD Read pages 90–96 to find out what happens when Rifka explores Antwerp.

Rifka explores the city. She gets lost.
Then a stranger helps her.

With freedom's seed the desert sowing,
I walked before the morning star . . .
—Pushkin

❧

March 17, 1920
Antwerp, Belgium

Dear Tovah,

Today I have met Antwerp. Even though it is still
winter, the air blew soft and mild today. All along
my walk back from the convent, windows were open.
Sounds from the houses drifted out into the street.

I took a different route home, turning down
one new lane, then another and another. I passed
millineries and bakeries and big department stores.

....

millineries women's hat stores

I passed barbers and markets and tailor shops.

I came to a café with heavy wooden doors **flung wide open**. Big green flowerpots sat on either side of the doorway and **a wild strange music streamed out from** the dark room. Most amazing of all, a giant man stood there, filling the doorway of the café. I had never seen **such a man** before. I thought my papa and my brothers were big, but they were nothing beside this man.

I must have been staring.

The giant looked down at me. He grinned—a grin so wide it was like the entrance to a tunnel. Inside that enormous mouth were teeth of pure gold!

I know you will not think this very clever of me, Tovah, but when I saw all those shining teeth in his huge dark mouth I was afraid. I turned and started running. I ran and ran until I could run no more. Leaning back against a low brick wall, I gasped for breath.

I didn't recognize anything.

....

flung wide open opened wide

a wild strange music streamed out from I could hear the wild and strange music that played in

such a man a man who looked like that

I tried to find my way back, but I couldn't.

The sun began to set and **the warmth of the day vanished**. A **brisk** wind blew through the streets, up the alleys, across the canals. I had not enough clothes on. I tried to keep myself from shaking, but the twilight chilled me. I was lost. I did not **have the least idea** how to get back to the house on King Street.

A milkman steered his horse and cart up the narrow street in the twilight. The cart clinked softly with empty bottles. I followed him, remembering Uncle Zeb and his horse, Lotkeh, and how Uncle Zeb would take me for rides when he didn't have business.

I did not know what this milkman would do to me if I stopped him. Uncle Zeb would have helped a lost child. But in Berdichev, if a Jew stopped the wrong person, they might **end up dead**.

I am not in Berdichev, I told myself. I am in Antwerp, and Sister Katrina and the lady from the HIAS have told me not to fear the people of Antwerp.

....

the warmth of the day vanished it got cold
brisk fast
have the least idea know
end up dead be killed

Well, I thought, if I am to **make it** back to my room tonight, I had better ask someone. So I called to the milkman sitting tall on his cart.

"Please," I asked. "Can you show me the way to King Street?"

He was tall and thin. He had a black mustache that hid his mouth altogether.

"Please," I said again, beginning in Flemish, finishing in Yiddish. "I am very . . . lost."

As he climbed down out of his cart he smiled at me. I could tell he smiled by the way his mustache lifted around his chin.

He **took** my face in his long fingers and smiled down at me.

"King Street?" he asked. "Come." The milkman clicked softly to his horse.

"My uncle drove a cart," I said, **jabbering nervously** as he walked me through the streets of Antwerp. "His horse's name was Lotkeh. I don't know where Lotkeh is anymore. Bubbe Ruth sold him after my uncle's death."

....

make it get

took held

jabbering nervously talking quickly because I was scared

The milkman led his horse with one hand. He offered me his other. I **hesitated** for a moment, then took it.

"My uncle used to take me for rides in his cart when he had no customers," I chattered in a mixture of Flemish and Yiddish, gripping the milkman's hand tightly. "Not that I don't like walking. I don't mind walking at all."

The milkman nodded, even though he could not understand all I said to him.

"It is very nice of you to help me," I said. "My uncle was nice, too. I think maybe you are a lot like him. My uncle was a very patient man."

The milkman glanced down at me. His mustache hairs tickled his bottom lip. His eyes were two warm coals in his long face. It felt good to be talking to him, holding his hand like I would hold Papa's, or Uncle Avrum's, or Uncle Zeb's.

The milkman not only took me back to King Street, which I can only think was **well out of his way**.

....

hesitated stopped

well out of his way far from where he was going

He took me to my very own door on King Street.

Tovah, he did not look like Uncle Zeb, except for the kindness in his eyes, but still, while I was with him, I felt Uncle Zeb near me. Outside the door of my house in Antwerp, the milkman bowed to me **in parting**.

I would not let go of his hand. There were hairs along the back of it, stiff dark hairs. I do not know why, Tovah, but I took that long hand of the milkman and pressed it to my lips. I kissed the strong, **leathery** hand of the milkman, right out in front of the house on King Street.

I never had a chance to say good-bye to Uncle Zeb. The soldiers shot him as he came out of his house. That was that. Kissing the hand of the milkman, I felt at last I could say good-bye to Uncle Zeb, too.

The milkman bowed to me once again. Then he lifted his long legs into his cart and he drove away.

It is late now. My candle burns low. I wonder, Tovah. How do you thank people for such kindness?

....

in parting as he left
leathery rough

I never knew strangers could be so kind. Do you think my brothers Asher and Reuben and Isaac would have done as much? I hope so.

Shalom, my dear cousin,
Rifka

BEFORE YOU MOVE ON...

1. **Cause and Effect** Rifka got lost. Reread page 91. What caused Rifka to lose her way?

2. **Conclusions** Reread pages 92–94. Why did Rifka trust the milkman?

LOOK AHEAD Who else does Rifka meet in Antwerp? Read pages 97–103 to find out.

Rifka begins to like Antwerp. She meets new people.
She shops and tastes new foods.

. . . And I shall know some savor of elation
Amidst the cares, the woes, and the vexation . . .
—Pushkin

July 29, 1920
Antwerp, Belgium

Dear Tovah,

Antwerp is a wonderful city. The people are so kind and generous, even the children.

I play with them in the park outside my room. Gizelle is the name of the girl who reminds me of Hannah. She really isn't like Hannah at all, now that I've come to know her. She is more **practical and solid** than Hannah. She brings her ball to the park

---

practical and solid useful and calm

and we play catch. I have learned many bouncing rhymes though I don't always understand what I am singing. The children laugh at my accent, but not in a cruel way.

It seems I have lived in Antwerp always. The old couple I **board** with, Marie and Gaston, are kind to me. They enjoy when I speak with them in Flemish. Gaston laughs and claps his hands when I tell him a story about my day. "Listen to her, Marie," he **crows**. "Is she not wonderful?"

I can hardly believe that it ever felt strange to me here. The bridges over the canals, the market at the Grunaplatz, the beautiful carriages and horses trotting along the streets, the cabarets and the hula dancers, they are all so familiar to me now. I wish Mama and Papa were here. The boys, too. And you, Tovah, and Hannah and Uncle Avrum and Bubbe Ruth, everyone, I wish you were all here. How I would love to share this wonderful city with you.

Not only are the people kind in Belgium, but the food is **splendid**. Sister Katrina and the lady from

....

board stay, live
crows says with a happy voice
splendid very good

the HIAS have introduced me to so many new tastes. Almost always, I eat in the market. It costs very little, so I am saving Papa's money, and **the food, Tovah, you wouldn't believe**. There is a fruit called a banana, colored yellow like a June sun and curved. You peel the skin off and underneath is a white fruit so sweet and creamy, it makes even Frusileh's milk seem thin by comparison.

And ice cream! If the people in Berdichev could taste ice cream, they would **give up** eating everything else. In the afternoon, the ice cream man comes down King Street with a giant dog pulling his cart.

He rings a little bell as he walks and we crowd around him. The dog wags its tail and stands very still. I never knew such a dog and such a man.

And there is chocolate. This food I found without anyone's help. Belgian chocolate. It is like biting off a little corner of heaven—even better than Mama's pastry, **may she never hear me say that**.

....

the food, Tovah, you wouldn't believe it is hard to believe how good the food is

give up stop

may she never hear me say that but I hope she never hears me say that

I told Sister Katrina how much I like the chocolate. Now she always has a piece for me to eat with the tea she serves after my treatment.

"You must eat foods that are good for you, too, Rifka," she says. "Not just chocolate."

"I know," I answer, but often I eat nothing but ice cream, and chocolate, and bananas. See, Tovah, I am a little clever. I have found one **advantage to being on my own**. I eat exactly **as I please**.

Sister Katrina says the ringworm is beginning to heal. She is happy with my progress, but I can tell she worries that there is no hair yet.

In Antwerp, it doesn't seem to matter that I have no hair. When I first arrived, the lady from the HIAS took me shopping. She took me to a department store and helped me choose some dresses.

I needed new clothes. The Belgians fumigate all your belongings before they let you enter their country, just as the Polish do. Of course the Belgians are far more kind in the way they treat you. But

....

advantage to being on my own good thing about being alone
as I please what I want

after two fumigations, my old clothes were **falling to pieces**.

While I was shopping with the lady from the HIAS that first week, I saw a hat that I wanted, a hat that would cover my baldness. I thought if I only owned such a hat, it would not matter so much that I was bald . . . but I did not have the money.

So I started saving, and as soon as I could, I returned to the department store. I would have that hat. With that hat I would not be ashamed of the way I look. With that hat I could hold my head up anywhere. But when I got to the store, the hat was gone. Sold to someone else.

"We can make you another," said the salesclerk. She **took my measurements** without saying a word about the scabs on my head. A new hat was made, just for me.

It is black velvet with shirring. The brim has light blue velvet underneath. Now that the ringworm is clearing up, I don't have to wear kerchiefs all the

....

falling to pieces too old and ripped to wear
took my measurements measured my head

time. I don't have to **sterilize** every stitch of cloth that comes near my head. I don't have to look like a poor, needy immigrant Jew from Berdichev.

I'm hoping I can go to America soon. Sometimes I think I will lose my mind longing for Mama, her yeasty hands, her red-cheeked face. And Papa, wrapped in his tallis, **davening**, his knees bent slightly, his body bobbing forward and back, praying in the gray light of dawn. I ache to smell the **kindled** Sabbath candles and to hear Papa and Mama's voices raised in prayer. Just to hold them and be held by them once more. I miss them so much. And the way Nathan brushed my hair. How he smoothed my tangled curls more gently than Mama ever did. I miss even Saul, and his big feet and his teasing.

I wonder if I can learn to make ice cream when I get to America. I know it has something to do with the milk from a cow. Maybe Bubbe Ruth and Frusileh can go into business. The Russians don't forbid Jews to make ice cream, yet. At least not that I know.

....

sterilize clean the germs from
davening praying
kindled burning

Maybe Bubbe Ruth can earn enough money making ice cream; she can be as **well-to-do** as you and Hannah and Uncle Avrum.

If I can't get you and Bubbe out of **the Old World**, maybe I can at least give to you something from **the new**.

Shalom, my cousin,
Rifka

....

well-to-do wealthy and successful
the Old World Russia
the new America

BEFORE YOU MOVE ON...

1. **Character** Rifka became friends with the children she used to watch at the park. How else have her feelings about Belgium changed?

2. **Character's Motive** Reread pages 102–103. Why did Rifka want to learn to make ice cream?

LOOK AHEAD Read pages 104–109 to find out if Rifka can go to America.

The ringworm is cured. Rifka can finally go to America. But her hair is not growing back.

. . . The sister of misfortune, Hope,
In the under-darkness dumb
Speaks joyful courage to your heart:
The day desired will come. . . .
—Pushkin

September 14, 1920
Antwerp, Belgium

Dear Tovah,

I am going to America! The nun, Sister Katrina, says my ringworm is completely cured, and the doctor signed my papers. "**Godspeed**," he said. "Go ahead."

At last I am free to go to America, to join Mama and Papa and all my giant brothers. It has been an

....

Godspeed Good luck

entire year since leaving Berdichev. Such a year!

My hair still has not started growing. Sister Katrina says perhaps it never will. I can't imagine going through life with no hair on my head. There are wigs, perukes, but a short, ugly peruke on my head? **What a thought!**

My hair was the only nice thing about me. Still, I am trying to remember your advice, Tovah, to **rely on my wits** and not my looks. I don't look so bad in a hat or with my kerchief, not really, **once you get used to it**. I hope Mama can get used to it. As for my being clever . . . even with what Sister Katrina and the lady from the HIAS say about me and languages, I'm still not so sure.

The lady from the HIAS helped me to buy my ticket. She looks very much like the HIAS lady in Warsaw: little and energetic, with an unruly silver bun on top of her head. Maybe they must all look like this to work for the HIAS. Maybe I should also work for the HIAS when I grow up. I am certainly the right

....

What a thought! I don't like to think about that!

rely on my wits use my intelligence

once you get used to it after you have seen me without hair a few times height. Though I might have difficulty with the bun if my hair does not grow.

The HIAS lady took me around to the steamship company as soon as the doctor gave me permission to leave. She advised me to buy a ticket on a small ship leaving Antwerp tomorrow. I could wait for two more weeks and sail on a big ship, but I don't want to wait. Besides, if I sailed on the big ship, I would have to sail to America in steerage. Steerage is what they call it when all the poor people crowd together down in the **belly** of the ship. People in steerage have no privacy, not an inch of space to turn from their left to their right. That is how Mama and Papa went across the ocean, and from the way they described it in their letter, I wouldn't like it very much at all. The rich people on such boats travel in **first class or second class**, but the poor people travel in steerage.

So I bought my ticket on a ship that has no classes. All the people traveling to America on this ship are equal. It is very democratic. "Democratic" is one of

....

belly bottom
first class or second class the nicest rooms

the words the lady from the HIAS has taught me.

I have been learning English. The HIAS lady brings me books and tutors me. Once she took me to an American movie about Tom Mix. Tom Mix is a cowboy, Tovah. Do you know what that is? He rides around on a horse all the time and shoots at bad people. I think Tom Mix loves his horse as much as Uncle Zeb loved Lotkeh.

I remember Uncle Zeb now like he was in a dream. So many new things fill my life, Tovah. I need to remind myself of how we **struggled** in Berdichev.

If it were not for the Pushkin, and for these letters to you, I would sometimes think I had dreamed all the terrible things about Russia. But when I read the Pushkin, I know my memories are real.

This morning I said good-bye to my friends in the park, especially Gizelle. I have decided to bring a present to Sister Katrina, to thank her for all she has done. She loves flowers. I will go to the market at the Grunaplatz and buy her the most beautiful **bouquet**

....

struggled had a difficult life
bouquet bunch of flowers

I can find. I have money. Papa has been sending it to me **all along**, and except for some food and clothes, I have **spent very little**. Tonight, Marie and Gaston have planned for me a little party.

Tovah, when I get to America, an entire ocean will **stand between** us. Until now I could have come back to Berdichev, not safely, but still, I could have come back. Only land separated us.

Now there will be this great ocean between us. I can't swim across an ocean to get back to Berdichev. And you know something, Tovah? I don't want to.

I will work in America and find a way to do everything, everything, just as I told the Polish girl on the train from Motziv.

Maybe when I write and tell you how wonderful America is, you will change your mind and come too, bringing the rest of our family with you out of Russia. Then we will all be together again. Aunt Anna, Uncle Avrum, Hannah, Bubbe Ruth, everyone.

....

all along while I've been here
spent very little not spent much money
stand between separate

But especially you, Tovah.

Tovah and Rifka. Imagine it. Two clever girls in the United States of America.

Shalom, my dear cousin,
Rifka

BEFORE YOU MOVE ON...

1. **Conclusions** Reread page 104. Why did the doctor sign Rifka's papers?

2. **Paraphrase** Reread page 107. Use your own words to tell why Pushkin and her letters were important to Rifka.

LOOK AHEAD Read pages 110–117 to find out how Rifka feels about the sailor she meets on the ship.

Rifka sails on a ship to America. She meets a young sailor. The sailor says she is clever and nice.

We numbered many in the ship,
Some spread the sails, some pulled, together,
The mighty oars; 'twas placid weather.
The rudder in his steady grip,
Our helmsman silently was steering
The heavy galley through the sea,
While I, from doubts and sorrows free,
Sang to the crew . . .

—Pushkin

❧

September 16, 1920
Somewhere on the Atlantic Ocean

Dear Tovah,
    The ship is excellent. I have a little room with a
bed **bolted** to the floor and a table that folds out.

....

bolted nailed, attached

A small round window looks out over the sea.

But who wants to **stay shut up in a cabin** when there is so much to do? **Such a lounge there is**, with a player piano and polished wooden counters. The lounge reminds me of your **salon** back in Berdichev, only much larger.

There are dances at night and the passengers **whirl about** on the parquet floor. During the day, a young sailor named Pieter puts brushes on his feet and he dances all alone, polishing and waxing. As he works, he sings and tells jokes to me.

Out on the deck are chairs for days of reading. They are bolted down like my bed so they won't **shift in heavy seas**. Of course we've had nothing like heavy seas since we boarded. Just clear skies and a gentle breeze.

"Sometimes," Pieter says, "there are storms so fierce I think the ship will break apart."

Pieter is such a joker. I am never certain whether

---

stay shut up in a cabin stay in a room and not go outside
Such a lounge there is There is a nice room for everyone
salon living room
whirl about dance
shift in heavy seas move when the sea is stormy

to believe him or not.

We trade songs and Pieter teaches me little dances when he is not **on watch**. He is like another brother to me. Only he is better somehow than a brother, though he teases every bit as much as Saul does. But it doesn't annoy me when Pieter teases. I like it.

If I sit down in one of these chairs with our Pushkin, Pieter rushes over and tucks a blanket around my legs.

"Is there anything else I can do for you, Miss Rifka?" he asks.

He treats me like a little **czarina**. Me, Rifka Nebrot. Sometimes I pinch myself. Only in Hannah's games did I feel so special. How Hannah would love this. Tovah, you would, too.

The ocean is so big; everywhere you look in every direction **swells this dark, billowing water**. It rises and falls as if it were breathing, and the ship **skates over the surface**.

I worried that perhaps I would feel seasick. I

---

on watch working

czarina wife of a Russian ruler

swells this dark, billowing water dark water moves and rises

skates over the surface moves smoothly over the ocean

heard so many stories, and some others on the ship complain, but I do not feel the least bit ill. I feel healthier than I have ever felt in my entire life—even if I don't have any hair on my head.

Today I had the most interesting conversation with Pieter. He had a few minutes before he went on duty and we walked around the deck, talking. He told me he had nine brothers.

"No sisters?" I asked.

"No," he said. "Mama **kept looking for** a girl, but we kept coming out boys."

I told him about Isaac and Asher and Reuben and Nathan and Saul.

"And then there is me," I said.

"All those sons and then a daughter," Pieter said. "You are **a treasure** to your mama and papa. And to your brothers."

"I've never met my brothers Isaac and Asher and Reuben," I told Pieter. "They left for America before I was born. So I don't know if I am a treasure to them.

....

kept looking for wanted to have
a treasure special

But I assure you I am no treasure to my brother Saul. To Nathan maybe, but not to Saul."

Can you imagine, Tovah? Me, a treasure? I told Pieter, "Really, I don't believe anyone in my family thinks of *me* as a treasure."

Pieter said, "If this is true, then your family is blind."

I lowered my eyes **for modesty's sake**, but I couldn't help the smile **that tugged at my lips**, Tovah.

Pieter said, "You are such a brave girl, Rifka.

And so clever to have **managed on your own**."

I had told him about our escape from Berdichev, and about the typhus, and how Mama and Papa had to leave me behind.

"I would not be so clever," Pieter said. "To learn so many languages. You speak Flemish better than I do and I have lived in Belgium all seventeen years of my life."

Again with the languages, Tovah. Why do people always **make such a to-do**?

....

for modesty's sake because I felt shy

that tugged at my lips on my face

managed on your own lived by yourself

make such a to-do think I am special for knowing languages

"Pieter," I said. "You are full of nice words, but I am not certain I deserve them. You call me brave, but I will tell you what is brave. My aunt Anna is brave, and my little grandmother. They are brave to stay in Russia and live with the hatred for the Jews. They are clever, too, so much more clever. In Berdichev, you must be clever simply to stay alive.

"For me, since I've left Berdichev, life has been easy, except that I have been apart from Mama and Papa. **I have met with such kindness.** No, I am not so brave, Pieter. If I were brave, I would have stayed in Russia."

"Maybe," Pieter said, "maybe they are very brave, the ones you have left behind in your homeland. But are they clever?"

"My cousin Tovah is very clever," I told Pieter. "She has chosen to stay."

"I'm a simple boy," Pieter said. "I can't learn the **speech** of other countries the way you can. I only travel back and forth across this big ocean. I do not

....

I have met with such kindness. People have been so nice to me.

speech languages

know much. But to me, Rifka, you seem very brave and very clever indeed."

Then Pieter bent over and kissed me! Right on my lips, Tovah. A warm kiss, with the soft blond hairs of his mustache tickling me.

Just for a moment I hoped the ship would never arrive in America and I could go on sailing with Pieter across this wide green ocean forever.

But when I looked up, Pieter's face was red. "I have work to do," he said, **stammering**. He hurried away, leaving me standing on the deck.

I don't understand. What did I do that Pieter should run away? How clever can I be, Tovah? The more I know, the more confused I get.

I returned to my cabin and opened our Pushkin. I tried to find a poem that said what I was feeling. Sometimes, when I read Pushkin's poems, I want to write poems of my own. I wonder if I **dare to do such a thing**. Saul always said I talked and talked without anything to say. But sometimes I do have something

....

stammering speaking quickly and nervously
dare to do such a thing am brave enough to do that

to say, and I feel as if I will explode if I don't write down what **is in my head and in my heart**.

Soon I will be in New York City, America. Soon I will be with Mama and Papa and all my giant brothers, Nathan and Saul, and Isaac and Asher and Reuben, brothers I don't even know.

In America, maybe, I will write poems.

Shalom, my cousin,
Rifka

....

is in my head and in my heart I am thinking and feeling

BEFORE YOU MOVE ON...

1. **Conclusions** Reread page 112. Why did Rifka sometimes pinch herself when Pieter was around?

2. **Inference** Reread page 116. Why do you think Pieter quickly left after he kissed Rifka?

LOOK AHEAD Read pages 118–127 to find out if Pieter and Rifka survive a terrible storm.

A bad storm starts. People on the ship are in great danger. Pieter saves Rifka's life. The ship is stuck in the Atlantic Ocean.

. . . When suddenly,
A storm! And the wide sea was rearing . . .
The helmsman and the crew were lost.
No sailor by the storm was tossed
Ashore—but I, who had been singing.
I chant the songs I loved of yore,
And on the sunned and rocky shore
I dry my robes, all wet and clinging.
—Pushkin

❧

September 21, 1920
Atlantic Ocean

Dear Tovah,

I have lost so much already, and now it seems I must lose more.

I **nearly drowned at sea** in a horrible storm. But I am alive. Everyone did not have my luck. But I am alive.

Our ship, which seemed so large and safe when first I boarded, barely survived **the fury of this storm**.

The **tempest** started during the night while we slept. I had dreams of **pogroms**, of cossacks on their horses, snapping whips at me, pointing rifles. I heard the crack of gunshot. In my dream the countryside was burning. I trembled in your cellar while the fire raged around me.

I woke from one terror into another. I had been thrown to the floor of my cabin, tossed from my bed by the rising seas.

Quickly I pulled on my clothes, tying my kerchief with trembling fingers. I opened my cabin door. Though it was still night, the sky was a sickly yellow, like an old bruise. I bashed against the ship's walls,

....

nearly drowned at sea almost died in the ocean
the fury of this storm the dangerous storm
tempest storm
pogroms large groups of people being killed

flung back and forth by the tossing sea as I **made my way** toward the deck. The ship shivered in the hateful ocean. Twice the floor dropped beneath me suddenly, and I fell.

There was so much confusion on deck. No rain yet, but a wind that roared. The seas, which had seemed so gentle yesterday, rose like hungry beasts, mouths open, hovering and crashing over the sides of the ship.

Sailors ran like spiders, back and forth in the yellow light. They yelled to each other over the wind, shouting directions. Pieter, my Pieter, **clung to a pillar as a wave broke over his shoulders**.

All the horrors of Russia returned to me. The storm frightened me as much as any pogrom, when the peasants would come after the Jews to burn our homes, to break into our stores, to murder us.

My stomach twisted and I knew I would be sick, so I crawled, making my way with difficulty, toward the side of the ship. The ship rolled, my stomach rolled with it. I clung to the rail, trying to raise up

....

made my way tried to walk

clung to a pillar as a wave broke over his shoulders held a pole when a wave hit him off my knees so I would not **soil myself** with my own sickness. The ship **plummeted** from beneath me and I hit my head on the metal rail.

Someone came up behind me and wrapped a blanket around my shoulders.

"Pieter!" I cried.

I didn't realize the waves had **drenched me**.

"Come, Rifka!" Pieter yelled over the wind. "You must come away from the side."

I started shivering. I could taste blood in my mouth and smell it in my nose. It had a cold, metallic taste that made my stomach twist inside out. I tore away from Pieter's grip and ran back to the rail, **emptying my stomach** over the side.

Before I could finish, water, a wall of water, rose up over me. Pieter grabbed me around the waist and hurled me away from the side. The water came crashing down over our heads, slamming us onto the deck.

Pieter held on to me as the water sucked at my

....

soil myself get myself dirty
plummeted fell very quickly
drenched me made me very wet
emptying my stomach vomiting

body, trying to pull me overboard. If he had not been there, Tovah, **the ocean would have claimed me**. He saved my life. Pieter held me until the wave lost its power and slipped away. Then he lifted me to my feet again before another monstrous wave could attack us.

"Come," he cried, guiding me toward a **hatch**. "Quickly. You must stay down **in the hold** while the storm lasts." Pieter shouted over the violent wind.

I descended into the ship's hold, looking up once at my friend. His hair lay plastered against his head and water streamed from his storm clothes.

"Pieter," I called, "are you putting me in steerage?"

Pieter laughed. "Brave and clever!" he called down to me. The wind screamed around him.

"Be careful, Pieter!" I cried.

"I will, Rifka," he answered.

I could hear the fear under the calm in his voice. It echoed in my ears as I stumbled down the ship's steep steps.

When I reached the bottom of the stairs, I found

....

the ocean would have claimed me I would have fallen into the ocean and died

hatch door in the boat's floor

in the hold below

many of the other passengers already in the hold, huddled together. We were still equal. We were equally miserable, equally frightened for our lives.

Everyone got sick, even me. It stank worse than a flood of soured milk down there.

Women rocked back and forth weeping. Men held their stomachs and moaned. All the time I worried for Pieter and the others. I **doubted**, Tovah, that I would live to see my family again.

If I'd had the Pushkin, I could have read from it. I could have opened it to the pages that held my golden Star of David, woven from broom straws, and prayed for our lives on it. But the Pushkin remained above, in my cabin, and I could not go after it.

We shivered and sweated and **retched** for thirty-six hours, until the ship stopped **its pitching**. At last the hatch was opened and we climbed up out of our hole.

There was no more deck left to the ship. Everything once bolted down had been ripped away.

....

doubted did not believe
retched vomited
its pitching moving back and forth

The player piano had crashed against a wall and shattered into pieces.

Most of the deck chairs were gone, too, torn right out of the floor. Twisted metal and bolts stuck up as signs of where the chairs had been.

The parquet tiles, what remained of them, were thick with filth from the sea.

A sailor lay on the deck, wrapped in gauze from head to toe, moaning. **My heart jumped into my throat.** What if it's Pieter? I thought. Oh, Tovah, if only I'd known.

I ran to the sailor's side, but it wasn't Pieter.

I asked if there was something I could do for him anyway. He didn't answer.

Other sailors were **limping** or bandaged. I looked for Pieter everywhere, but I couldn't find him.

Finally I stopped one of the officers.

"Have you seen the boy, Pieter?" I asked. "Please, I know you are busy, but could you tell me where I might find him?"

My heart jumped into my throat. I was very scared.
limping walking with difficulty

The officer looked down at me. He steadied my shoulders in his hands the way Papa had the night he told me of Uncle Zeb's death. "We lost one sailor overboard in the storm," he said.

"Pieter?" I whispered.

The officer nodded.

Tovah, **I felt myself smothering**. I couldn't see anything, hear anything.

Somehow I found my way back to my cabin, and for the first time since leaving Berdichev, I cried. All the tears that had collected in this year, in this enormous year, shoved their way out of my heart, and how I cried.

Pieter, who said I was so brave . . . what would he say to see me now?

I didn't care. I cried for Pieter, I cried for myself. I couldn't stop. I didn't want to stop.

I cried until I **was empty of** tears. Then I was still. As still as the sea after a storm.

I sit in my cabin and wait. Our ship has sent out

I felt myself smothering I felt like I could not breathe
was empty of had no more

a **distress call**. It cannot move anymore **on its own steam**. The drum of the engines had been like a heartbeat. Now the heart has stopped. The engines are dead.

We must wait for another ship to answer our signal and tow us across the ocean to America. I pray there are no more storms between now and then. We could never survive another fight with the sea.

Tovah, suddenly I feel how **defenseless** we are—not just Jews, all of us. My mind fills with images of you and Aunt Anna and Bubbe Ruth and Mama and Papa. I see Bubbe Ruth at the rear of the long house, huddled beside her little stove, sipping tea from the samovar. I see Papa and Mama swallowed up by a strange country called America. I see you, Tovah, staring out the window at the empty road, the road that has carried me away from you. I realize how **precious** our lives are. And how brief. I want to come home.

....

distress call call for help
on its own steam by itself
defenseless helpless
precious special, important

The telegram the HIAS sent from Antwerp to Mama and Papa said I would be arriving in America today. Today I sit in the middle of the Atlantic Ocean on a ship that is dead.

What will happen when Papa and Mama come to get me and I'm not there? How will they know when to come back? Will I ever see them again?

I'm too tired, Tovah, too tired **for all this trouble**. At this moment I wish I had never left Berdichev.

Shalom, my Tovah,
Rifka

---

for all this trouble from everything that has happened

BEFORE YOU MOVE ON...

1. **Character** Reread pages 124–125. Rifka heard that Pieter died in the storm. Why did Rifka cry for Pieter and for herself?

2. **Summarize** Reread page 126. What did Rifka learn about life?

LOOK AHEAD Read pages 128–131 to find out if the ship makes it to America.

The ship gets closer to Ellis Island in America.
Rifka is sure she will see her family soon.

. . . And thoughts stir bravely in my head, and rhymes
Run forth to meet them on light feet, and fingers
Reach for the pen . . .
—Pushkin

❦

October 1, 1920
Entering New York Harbor

Dear Tovah,

Today we will arrive at Ellis Island. Today I will
see Mama and smell her yeasty smell. Today I will
feel the tickle of Papa's dark beard against my cheeks
and see my brother Nathan's dimpled smile and Saul's
wild curly hair. Today I will meet my brothers Asher
and Isaac and Reuben.

Already I am wearing my best hat, the black velvet with the shirring and the brim of light blue. I'm hoping that with the hat, Mama will not **mind** my baldness. I've **tucked** Papa's tallis into my rucksack, but Mama's gold locket hangs around my neck.

The captain said his company **notified our families** and they are awaiting our arrival. I must pass a **screening** on the island before I can go home with Mama and Papa. Papa wrote about Ellis Island in his letters.

He wrote that at Ellis Island you are neither in nor out of America. Ellis Island is a line separating my future from my past. Until I cross that line, I am still homeless, still an immigrant. Once I leave Ellis Island, though, I will truly be in America.

Papa said in his letter that they ask many questions at Ellis Island. I must take my time and answer correctly. What's to worry? I am good at answering questions. Even if they ask me a thousand

....

mind be sad about

tucked put away

notified our families told our families that we are coming

screening doctor's exam

questions, I will have Mama and Papa near me, my mama and papa.

Just one week ago, I did not think I would ever make it to America. We **drifted** on the sea for days, helpless, waiting for the ship to come and tow us. I assisted with the cleanup as best I could, doing work Pieter would have done if he were there.

Then, once the tow ship arrived it took so long between the securing of the ropes and the exchanges between the two ships, I thought we would never begin moving. At last, when we did, the other ship pulled us so slowly. I could swim faster to America.

In Russia, all America meant to me was excitement, adventure. Now, coming to America means so much more. It is not simply a place you go when you run away. America is a place to **begin anew**.

In America, I think, life is as good as a clever girl can make it.

Very soon, Tovah, I will be in this America. I hope someday you will come, too.

Shalom, my cousin,
Rifka

....

drifted floated; did not move forward
begin anew start a new life; begin again

P.S. As I was finishing this letter **a cry went up** from the deck. When I went out to see what it was, I found all the passengers gathered on one side of the ship, looking up. They were looking at **Miss Liberty**, Tovah, a great statue of a woman standing in the middle of the harbor. She was lifting a lamp to light the way for us.

....

a cry went up I heard people shouting
Miss Liberty the Statue of Liberty

BEFORE YOU MOVE ON...

1. **Context Clues** Reread page 129. The ship arrived at Ellis Island. Rifka's papa wrote: "at Ellis Island you are neither in nor out of America." What does this mean?

2. **Comparisons** How have Rifka's feelings changed from the last letter?

LOOK AHEAD Read pages 132–138 to find out why a chalk mark is terrible news for Rifka.

**Rifka must stay on Ellis Island until her hair grows.
A woman from HIAS tries to help Rifka.**

---

*. . . Give me your hand. I will return
At the beginning of October . . .*
—Pushkin

ॐ

October 2, 1920
Ellis Island

Dear Tovah,

I don't know how to tell about what has happened.
I feel numb and I can't believe. I thought if I could
tell you, maybe it would make some sense, maybe it
would help.

They are holding me, detaining me on Ellis Island,
at the hospital for **contagious diseases**. They won't let
me go to Mama and Papa. They won't even let me see

....

contagious diseases sicknesses that people give to each other them. Tovah, I can't go to America!

After we **landed**, I sat on a bench in an enormous room with hundreds of others, waiting to hear my name called.

I waited a long time. I just wanted to see Mama and Papa. I kept looking around for them, for Mama's black hair, for Papa's beard, but they weren't there. There were others with thick beards, with dark hair, but they weren't my mama and papa. Certainly I would know my own mama and papa.

Finally a man called my name. I couldn't understand what he said to me. I felt nervous and he spoke English so fast, much faster than the lady from the HIAS. Someone found an interpreter for me. I answered their questions, I read from a book to prove I am not a **simpleton**, but they kept delaying my approval.

The doctor examined me. He took off my hat, my beautiful hat. I didn't like his taking off my hat any more than I liked the Russian guard touching my hair

....

landed got off the boat
simpleton stupid person

or the Polish doctor examining me at the border, but just as then, I **had no choice**.

The first doctor called over another doctor. They spoke fast. They looked at my scalp. They shook their heads. Then they called for a tall man with glasses. The nosepiece was dull with the mark of his thumbprint, so often did he shove the gold rims up on his thin nose.

"What is it?" I asked, pulling on the doctors' sleeves, but they didn't answer. The first doctor put a chalk mark on my shoulder and pointed me in the direction of a cage holding the detainees.

Detainees are immigrants who are not welcome in America. They remain on the island until the **authorities** decide what to do with them. People like criminals and simpletons are detainees. I didn't belong with them. I could not belong with them.

"Why are you holding me?" I cried in Yiddish. "Why have you put me with these people? I don't belong here. I belong in America. I have come

----

had no choice could not stop him

authorities people who decide whether immigrants can come into the United States to America."

A lady from the HIAS came over. She, too, was short, like the HIAS lady in Antwerp and the HIAS lady in Warsaw, but this one had a red bun on the top of her head.

"**Shah**," she said. "Don't make such a fuss. If you **calm down**, I will help you."

She spoke with the doctor. She spoke with the man who wore the gold-rimmed glasses. I saw her face grow less and less hopeful. When she walked back to me, I could tell it was not good news.

She explained to me in Yiddish what the doctors had said. "You must be kept in the hospital for contagious diseases. It's because of the ringworm you suffered from in Europe."

"They cured my ringworm!" I cried.

"Mr. Fargate, the tall man with the glasses, says he must be certain the ringworm is gone before you can enter the country," the lady from the HIAS said. "Perhaps it will only take a day or two."

....

Shah Be quiet
calm down are calm and stop shouting

"A day or two. I must go to Mama and Papa now! My papers say the ringworm is cured!" I cried. "Why don't they believe my papers? Why must I wait?"

"It's not just the ringworm that concerns them," said the lady from the HIAS. "It's your hair." She stroked my cheek with the back of her hand. She had a brown wart on her chin, with red hairs growing out of it. I pulled back from her.

"My hair?" I asked. I tugged at the black velvet hat, pulling it down until it nearly covered my ears.

"The doctors worry about your hair."

"Why should they worry over such a thing as my hair?" I asked.

"To them it is important," the HIAS lady said. "Even though your ringworm may be gone, if your hair does not grow back, Rifka, the American government will have to **view** you as a social responsibility."

"What does this mean? Social responsibility?" I asked.

"It means the American government is afraid they will have to **support you** for the rest of your life," the

....

view think of

support you pay for your food and other things you need

136

lady from the HIAS said. "Your lack of hair makes you **an undesirable immigrant**. They think without hair you will never find a husband to take care of you and so *they* will have to take care of you instead."

I couldn't believe what she was saying.

"Some Jewish women shave their heads **on purpose**," I said. "It is written into the Jewish law. To be bald is not a **sin**."

The HIAS lady sighed.

"You mean the country will not let me in simply because they are afraid when I grow up no one will want to marry me?"

"That is right."

"You don't need hair to be a good wife, do you?" I asked. "Jewish women wear wigs all the time. I could wear a wig and still be a good wife."

"You are a child," the lady from the HIAS said. "It is not that simple."

"It is that simple," I said.

She said, "I can't change the rules, Rifka. Either

....

an undesirable immigrant a person that they do not want to enter the United States

on purpose because they want to; not by accident

sin bad thing

your hair grows or they will send you back."

There it was. What chance did I have of my hair growing now? It had not grown in almost a year.

Tovah, I think maybe you were wrong after all. You said a girl must not depend on her looks, that it is better to be clever. But in America looks are more important, and if it is my looks I must rely on, I am to be sent back. How can this be?

Shalom,
Rifka

BEFORE YOU MOVE ON...

1. **Conclusions** Reread page 134. What did the chalk mark on Rifka's shoulder mean? How do you know?

2. **Cause and Effect** Reread pages 136–137. The American government did not want a woman without hair to come to America. Why?

LOOK AHEAD Read to page 147 to find out what Rifka does when she meets an enemy.

Rifka meets a Russian peasant boy in the hospital. He is starving. Rifka tries to help him.

===

> . . . My path is bleak—before me stretch my
> morrows:
> A tossing sea, foreboding toil and sorrows.
> And yet I do not wish to die, be sure;
> I want to live—think, suffer, and endure . . .
>
> —Pushkin

October 7, 1920
Ellis Island

Dear Tovah,

I have been here a week now. It is not so bad a place, really. I am growing used to it. Crowds of people **overfill the wards**. When they first brought me here, they gave me a choice. I could sleep in a bed

----

overfill the wards have to share the rooms and beds

with another woman or by myself, in a **crib**. I said, "I'll take the crib."

My feet stuck out one end, but it was better than sleeping with someone I didn't know. Someone who had a disease I didn't want. Sometimes it is **convenient** I am small.

There are so many of us here in the hospital. After two days, I was **transferred from one ward** to another. In the new ward, I got my own bed.

Saul came to visit, but they sent him to the first ward and he couldn't find me. No one could find me. So they sent Saul away.

Saul would have been the first familiar face in almost a year. I didn't care that it was just Saul. I would love to have seen Saul, but they sent him away.

When they did find me, they put me in still another ward. Here a nurse has taken an interest in me.

Her name is Nurse Bowen. Sometimes she takes me to her room in a building on a different part of

....

crib baby's bed

convenient good that

transferred from one ward moved from one part of the hospital

Ellis Island. We go in a little boat to get there. I help her clean her apartment. Mostly, though, I eat candy when I am there. She always has candy. It is not as good as Belgian chocolate, but still it tastes very good. I like going with her.

I **make better sense of** English now. I listen to the nurses and the doctors, following them **on their rounds of** the wards. I have been able, even, to interpret a little for the Polish and Russian patients; only simple things, but the nurses and the doctors seem pleased to have me help them.

There is a little Polish baby here. She has no one. Her mama died of the typhus. Because I've already had the disease, I help take care of her. She is such a beautiful little thing, with **dark eyes taking up half her face** and a bald head, as bald as mine. She never fusses. I hold her and rock her and sing her Yiddish lullabies. I tell her stories and recite Pushkin to her. She reminds me a little of the baby on the train in Poland.

....

make better sense of understand more
on their rounds of as they walk around
dark eyes taking up half her face big, dark eyes

I have another responsibility. In the dining hall one night, a little boy sat across from me at the table. I couldn't tell what was wrong with him, why they were keeping him in the hospital, except that he was very thin and pale, with dark circles under his eyes. I looked in those eyes and remembered something, someone, but I was too hungry **to give it much thought**.

They served the food. It's not bad food, and there is so much of it. Hands went **every which way**, passing, dishing out, spooning in. But the little boy sat, watching it all go past him.

I **helped myself to** potatoes and meat and carrots and bread. The boy stared at my plate, but he took nothing for himself.

"What's the matter with you?" I asked in Yiddish. "Why don't you eat?"

He didn't answer.

"Eat," I said in English.

Still no answer.

....

to give it much thought to think about it a lot

every which way everywhere

helped myself to took

"Take something to eat," I said in Russian.

Now he looked up at me, straight into my eyes.

"Russian you understand?" I said. "But not Yiddish?"

Then I knew. The boy was a peasant. A Russian peasant. Here, sitting before me, Tovah, was the reason we had fled our homeland. He was the reason for my being alone for so long, separated from my family. The reason I had had typhus. The reason I had lost my hair. The reason Uncle Zeb was dead and all your lives were in danger. I had him sitting in front of me in the dining hall of the hospital at Ellis Island.

I tried not to look at him. I did not want **anything to do with him**. But there he was, in front of me. A little Russian peasant.

He stared at his pale hands, folded in front of him at his place. Then he looked back up at me with those eyes.

I remembered then. He **looked like a small version** of the soldier at the train station, the one with the

------

anything to do with him to think about him or do anything to help him

looked like a small version made me think

eyes of green ice. I didn't want anything to do with him. Nothing.

But no one should starve to death, Tovah. Certainly not a little boy, maybe seven years old.

"Is there something wrong with you that **keeps** you from eating?" I asked in Russian.

He shook his head.

"If you don't eat," I told him, "they will send you back."

He nodded.

"You want to go back?" I asked.

He nodded again, and this time **tears filled his eyes.**

"Well, just tell them you want to go back!" I cried.

If I go back, they will kill me. His father or his uncle, his cousin or his neighbor, they will make a pogrom, and they will kill me.

Crazy Russian peasant! He could stay here. He could stay here in America. There is nothing wrong with him. He could live in either place, Russia,

....

keeps stops
tears filled his eyes he started crying

America, and no harm would come to him. But no, he is starving himself so they will send him back.

People were eating all around us. The boy sat at his empty plate, tears rolling down his cheeks.

I hated him. I hated what he **stood for**.

I also hated seeing him cry. He was just a little boy.

"What's your name?" I asked.

"Ilya," he answered. His voice came out thin and high and **frail**.

"Ilya," I said. "If you don't eat anything, you will grow so weak that when they do send you back, you will die before you reach home. You must eat a little,"

I stood up and looked for food to **spoon onto his plate**, but by now all the food bowls were empty.

What could I do? He was just a little boy, a hungry, frightened little boy. I lifted my plate and slid some of my own food onto his dish.

"Now eat," I said. "Or I will be hungry for nothing."

He put a little piece of carrot in his mouth and

....

stood for   made me think of

frail   weak

spoon onto his plate   put on his plate with my spoon

chewed. Then faster and faster he pushed the food in.

"Slow down," I said. "You'll get sick."

He finished everything on his plate, so I gave him a little more.

Maybe it is not very clever to feel what I felt about this Russian peasant, this enemy of my people.

But Tovah, he was just a little, hungry boy. Taking care of him made me feel better than I had felt in a very long time.

Ever since then, **I have a shadow**. He follows me everywhere, holding on to my skirts. He sits by me when I rock the Polish baby, though I will not let him come too close. He follows me around the buildings, he sits under my elbow at mealtime, he is always **under my feet**.

The nurses call me the little mother. I don't mind so much.

What do you think about your cousin taking care of a little Russian peasant? You will probably think me the most foolish of all, to **befriend** such a child. I

....

I have a shadow the boy follows me everywhere
under my feet close to me
befriend make friends with

know Mama will not be happy, not the way she feels about everything Russian. I must figure out a way to explain to her when she comes to visit.

Oh, Tovah, **how I hope she comes** to visit soon.

Shalom,
Rifka

....

how I hope she comes I want her

BEFORE YOU MOVE ON...

1. **Character's Motive** Reread pages 146–147. Rifka met a Russian peasant. At home he was the enemy. Why did she talk to him anyway?

2. **Cause and Effect** Why wasn't Ilya eating?

LOOK AHEAD Rifka finally sees someone from her family. Read pages 148–159 to find out who she sees.

Saul visits Rifka in the hospital. Ilya and Saul do not like each other. Rifka learns that her family is working very hard in America.

. . . I'm lean and shaven, but alive
. . . And there is hope that I may thrive. . . .
—Pushkin

❧

October 9, 1920
Ellis Island

Dear Tovah,

At last, I have seen someone from the family. I had started believing they weren't really here, that something terrible had happened to them and no one would tell me. I thought the Americans had **stolen them away and imprisoned them** and I would never see them again.

---

stolen them away and imprisoned them put them in jail

But Saul came. He **skipped school** and came to see me at the hospital.

"Mama and Papa and the others can't **get away**," he said in Yiddish. "They must all work. I thought I'd come."

Tovah, when I saw him—he's so big, so handsome—I almost cried.

But I wouldn't let Saul see me cry. He walked through the door and stood there, looking around the ward for me.

"Saul!" I called out. I ran to him and threw my arms around him.

He backed me away and looked down at me. "Rifka?"

"What's the matter?" I asked. "You don't recognize your own sister?"

He swallowed. I saw the knob in his big neck go up and down.

"You look different," Saul said. I touched the kerchief covering my bald head.

"My hair," I said. "It's been gone a long time."

....

skipped school did not go to school for the day

get away leave the place where they work

"No, it's not that," he said. "I don't remember your eyes being so big."

"I have the same eyes, Saul."

I **took my brother by the hand** and led him into the ward. I was glad to have a bed of my own when Saul came. It would embarrass me if he should learn I slept in a crib. He would never let me forget that.

"Here, I brought something for you." Saul reached into his pocket and brought out a banana. **His eyes twinkled with mischief.**

I took the banana and peeled it and started to bite into it. Then I remembered how he had shared with me in Motziv, and I offered him the first bite. He shook his head. The **sparkle** had gone from his eyes. He looked disappointed.

"What's the matter, Saul?" I asked.

"How did you know to do that?" Saul asked. "How did you know to peel the banana? In Russia, we didn't see bananas."

I laughed. "Is that what's worrying you? There are lots of bananas in Antwerp," I told him. "And

....

took my brother by the hand held my brother's hand

His eyes twinkled with mischief. He looked like he wanted to laugh at me.

sparkle secret look

chocolates, and ice cream, too."

"Humph," Saul said. "I guess you're not such a greenhorn."

"What's a greenhorn?" I asked.

"It's when you come off the boat and you don't know what a banana is," Saul said.

"Well, I guess I'm not a greenhorn, then."

Saul was **dressed like a dandy**. He wore knickers and a stiff shirt. **A cap sat cocked on his head.** He was showing off in front of me. He wanted me to say something nice about his clothes. But he had hoped to **make a fool of me** with that banana. I didn't want him to know how handsome I thought he looked. My American brother.

When Doctor Askin came by on his rounds, I spoke English, introducing the doctor to Saul.

Doctor Askin said, "It's a pleasure to meet you, young man."

Saul, my giant brother Saul, looked down at his big feet and said nothing. His ears turned red.

....

dressed like a dandy wearing nice clothes

A cap sat cocked on his head. He wore a cap pushed to one side of his head.

make a fool of me make me look stupid or silly

"Saul," I said, kicking his shoe with my boot. Still Saul said nothing.

"He is happy to meet you, too, Doctor Askin," I said. "Are you not, Saul?"

Saul nodded. Doctor Askin said good-bye and walked away.

"Doctor Askin is my friend," I told Saul, still speaking in English. "Why did you not talk to him? He is a good man. He brings the **comics** here. We look at the pictures. I can read a little."

"You *read* English, too?" Saul asked.

"A little," I said. "I am learning each day. Nurse Bowen helps. Doctor Askin helps, too, before he and Mr. Fargate talk about patients."

"Your English," Saul said, "is very good. Where did you learn to speak this way, Rifka? You learned this in Antwerp, too?"

"Yes," I told him. "I learned much in Antwerp."

Saul looked at me with his head tilted to one side. "My sister Rifka speaks like an American in one week?"

---

comics stories with pictures

"Nine days," I said. "I've been here nine days."

"**Smarty**," he said. He lifted his hand to **tousle my hair**, something he used to do when I had blond curls, back in Russia.

Saul pulled his hand back before he touched the kerchief hiding my bald head.

"What should I tell Mama about your hair?" he asked.

"Tell her the truth," I said. "It's not growing. Why should it grow now? It hasn't grown in a year."

Saul looked down at his feet. "So they will send you back?"

I didn't know what to say.

Saul looked so big and healthy and uncomfortable in the busy hospital ward. I smiled at him. "If I have to go back, Saul, I'm sure I can stay with Bubbe Ruth. Or Uncle Avrum and Tovah and Hannah. It won't be so bad for me."

Saul and I both knew the truth. We'd left Berdichev to save his life. Because of this, I might very well lose mine.

....

Smarty You're smart
tousle my hair move his fingers through my hair quickly

Just then, Ilya appeared, **wiggling his way** under my arm. I introduced him to Saul in English. "This is my little friend," I said. "He also comes from Russia."

Saul noticed the book of Pushkin that Ilya pulled out from under my pillow. Ilya likes when I read Pushkin to him, especially in the afternoon when **things quiet down for a little while around the ward**.

"What **have you got there**?" Saul asked Ilya in Yiddish.

Ilya did not answer. He looked frightened of Saul.

Saul took the book from him.

Ilya's eyes flashed with anger.

"Ilya," I said in Russian. "This is my brother."

Ilya looked from me to Saul, but he is a stubborn little boy. He tried to get the book back from Saul. Between the two pulling on it, Tovah, the Pushkin dropped and fell open. My Star of David, the one I had woven from broom straws in Antwerp, bounced off the floor and broke apart.

....

wiggling his way moving himself

things quiet down for a little while around the ward the hospital room becomes calm and quiet

have you got there do you have

Ilya knew how precious the little straw star had been to me. Always, he had **handled it with such care**. He looked into my face, blinked his green eyes, and then ran out of the ward.

"He's a nasty little peasant," Saul said. "I don't believe you, Rifka. What are you doing with a peasant? And this book. Throw it away. It's a Russian book! And what is all this **scribbling** inside?"

"Leave it alone, Saul," I said, grabbing the book and holding it tight to my chest. I was angry at him. He had broken my star. But I was angry at him for more than that. Inside, it felt like much more than that.

"You can't tell me what I should throw away," I said. It hurt deep in my heart, Tovah, but at this moment I loved Ilya more than I loved my own brother. "This book, it's mine—"

Saul grabbed for the book again, but I **stood my ground**, squeezing the hard cover against my ribs.

"You're different, Rifka," Saul said.

....

handled it with such care held it carefully, so it would not break
scribbling writing
stood my ground would not let him have it

"I am the same, Saul," I cried. "Still, my life has **gone on** while we've been apart. I am older in many ways since you left me in Warsaw."

"You're still my little sister, though," Saul said.

Saul's dark eyes burned with anger, but something else burned there, too. I remembered Pieter and what he'd said about my being a treasure to my brothers.

I put my hand on Saul's sleeve. "Yes. I am still your little sister. Let's not fight, Saul. I have been so lonely. You haven't even told me anything about Mama or Papa or Nathan and the others. Please stay and talk with me."

Saul looked as if he was still angry, but he sat back down. My cot groaned under his weight.

"Papa and Mama work all day at the clothing factory," Saul said. "When they come home at night, they bring bags of **trousers to hem**. They work together until late. I help, but I can't stay awake so long to finish."

Mama and Papa—working so hard? They needed my help. Couldn't the Americans see how much my family needed me?

....

gone on continued
trousers to hem pants to sew

"What about Nathan?" I asked.

"Nathan has a job in a bakery. He leaves before light and comes home after dark, his clothes always covered with flour."

"And you?"

"I go to school," Saul said. "Papa says I must get an education. I'd rather be working, but Papa says no. If you were with us, Rifka, maybe he would let me work. Maybe it would be enough for you to go to school. But . . ."

Saul didn't finish. None of us **had any say** about whether I could come to join my family and go to an American school. I wanted nothing more than that.

But only Mr. Fargate could decide.

Saul said, "Isaac married a girl named Sadie. Sadie Chenowitz, of the Berdichev Chenowitzes."

What a small world, Tovah. My oldest brother, Isaac, comes all the way from Russia and who does he pick to marry but **a landsman**, a girl from our own village, **a Chenowitz girl**.

"She's very pretty," Saul said.

....

had any say could make the decision

a landsman a person who comes from the same country

a Chenowitz girl a girl from the Chenowitz family

He said Isaac and Sadie had a baby boy named Aaron.

"That makes me an aunt," I said, clapping my hands. "Can you believe it? Me, Aunt Rifka." I wanted to hold my brother Isaac's baby, right that instant.

"Did Mama ever get new candlesticks?" I asked.

Saul said they could not afford to buy candlesticks. He said everything they earned they sent to me in Belgium. My dear family, how much they had given up for me.

"What do you do on the Sabbath?" I asked.

"We work on the Sabbath," Saul said.

I couldn't believe my ears. Mama, Papa, working on the Sabbath?

I opened my rucksack and took out my pouch of money.

"Where did you get all this, Rifka?" Saul asked.

"I saved it," I said. "From the money Papa sent."

"Papa sent that money for you to eat, Rifka. What did you eat?"

"I ate, Saul," I said. I wasn't about to tell him *what* I ate.

"I want you to take this money, Saul," I said. "I want you to take it and buy candlesticks for Mama. If there is any money left, tell Mama and Papa to use it so they do not have to work on the Sabbath. Do you hear me, Saul?"

Saul promised about the candlesticks. He apologized for breaking my star. Then he was gone. I had forgotten how lonely I'd been until he was gone.

Tovah, I have never seen my brother Isaac. He fled Russia before I was born. Now I wonder if I ever will see him, or his baby. Would they send me back, do you think, without ever holding my brother's baby?

Shalom,
Rifka

BEFORE YOU MOVE ON...

1. **Inference** Reread pages 149–150. Saul visited Rifka. Why do you think Saul backed away and looked down at Rifka?

2. **Conclusions** Reread pages 151–152. Why didn't Saul talk to the doctor?

LOOK AHEAD Read pages 160–169 to find out what makes Rifka so happy.

Mama finally visits Rifka. She sees how much Rifka cares for others. Rifka worries about Ilya.

. . . They say ill things of the last days of Autumn:
But I, friend reader, not a one will hear;
Her quiet beauty touches me as surely
As does a wistful child, to no one dear. . . .
——Pushkin

October 11, 1920
Ellis Island

Dear Tovah,

Mama came today.

My wonderful, beautiful Mama. She hugged me and kissed me and **I smelled onion on her** and chicken and celery and yeast. I was so happy I thought my heart had broken open like an egg.

....

I smelled onion on her her skin smelled like onions

"Mama," I kept repeating, afraid I would blink and she would no longer be sitting beside me on my cot.

Mama brought out a tiny honey cake. "For your thirteenth birthday," she said in Yiddish.

She watched me eat it, the whole thing, as we sat close together on the edge of my bed. I licked each finger. It tasted as good as I remembered, Mama's honey cake.

"Tell me about Antwerp," Mama said.

I told her about Sister Katrina and the lady from the HIAS and Gizelle in the park. I told her about the awful storm at sea, and how our ship needed **towing** to Ellis Island.

"What about your hair?" Mama asked. "Is it really so bad?"

Mama led me over to the window and took off my kerchief. She examined my scalp. I felt envy for the long black hair coiled around her ears.

She sighed and rested her hand on my naked head.

"Please," I said, removing her hand.

....

towing to be pulled

I carefully tied the kerchief back on.

"I wish your bubbe were here," Mama said. "Your bubbe would know what to do."

"I wish she were here, too, Mama," I answered back.

I wish you were here, too, Tovah, but now I don't know if that is such a good idea. You have to be perfect to come to America. I have this bald head and you, you have a crooked back. We are not perfect. We are not welcome.

"These Americans," I told Mama. "**They don't make any sense.** They say they are holding me because I am too contagious to come into their country, but they allow you to visit me. If I'm contagious, won't I make you sick? And if I make you sick, won't you make everyone else in America sick? **What's the difference** if I go to New York or you come here? Either way, if I really am contagious, somebody is going to get sick. I'm wondering how clever these Americans really are."

....

They don't make any sense. I don't understand them.
What's the difference How is it different

"Hush, Rifka," Mama said. "Somebody could hear you."

I looked around. Even if they did speak Yiddish, no one around us was listening.

"Why is such a great country like America afraid of a little Jewish girl just because she doesn't have any hair on her head?" I said. "The truth, Mama, is that they're afraid I will never find a husband. As if I need hair to get married."

"Maybe we could rub something in to make your hair grow," Mama said. "I wish Papa could come. He would have some ideas."

"It's no good, Mama," I said. "Not even Papa can get my hair to grow. I am bald."

"But Rifka," Mama said.

Then she didn't say anything more. What could she say? I am bald.

"Don't worry, Mama."

Mama never was very good with **doctoring**. Always Papa nursed us through sickness.

---

doctoring helping people feel better when they were sick; acting like a doctor

"Are you eating right?" Mama wanted to know.

"The food is very good here."

I didn't tell her about all the chocolate and ice cream I ate in Belgium.

Doctor Askin came and said hello to Mama. Then he joined Mr. Fargate for the **case reviews**.

I was telling Mama about the market in Antwerp when my little Polish baby began crying.

"Excuse me, please, Mama," I said. I left Mama sitting on my bed. I didn't want to leave her. I didn't want to lose one precious second with her, but the baby needed me.

As soon as I settled the baby down, a **fevered** woman asked for water. Then there were other chores that **needed doing**, things I helped the nurses with every day. I kept looking over to Mama, afraid she would disappear.

She didn't disappear. She sat and watched.

"Just like Papa," she said when I finally got back to her. "And the way you speak English, Rifka. You've

....

case reviews meetings to decide which patients could enter America

fevered sick

needed doing I needed to do

always been good with languages. You were talking before you could walk. But I never imagined you could learn English so quickly. I have been here a year. I hardly speak a word."

"I could help you," I told Mama, "if they allow me to stay."

"Who is the baby?" Mama asked.

I took Mama's hand and led her over to the crib.

I said. "She is Polish. Her mother died of the typhus. The baby has the typhus, too. See." I showed Mama the rash. "I help take care of her."

Ilya, I noticed, **kept his distance the whole of Mama's visit**. Usually he clung to me like a drop of sap. He was even jealous when I held the baby.

Maybe Ilya understood something about Mama.

Tovah, you would be accepting of my friendship with Ilya. Uncle Avrum has Russian friends, non-Jewish friends. But Mama and Papa, they wouldn't like it at all.

Mama can be more **accepting** of the Polish baby.

....

kept his distance the whole of Mama's visit did not come near me while Mama visited

accepting understanding

A baby that speaks no language. It could be a Jewish baby, after all. There are many Polish Jews. But Ilya is no Jew. He is a Russian peasant, and Mama and Papa have grown to hate everything Russian.

I have been thinking, Tovah. To **turn my back on** the part of me that is Russian is impossible. I am Jewish, yes, but I am Russian, too. I am both Jewish and Russian. And I am also more. I am so much more.

When I read the poetry of Pushkin to Ilya and watch his face, I can see the words rocking him the way they do me. We both ache for something we have lost.

Yet he aches in a way that I cannot imagine. At least I still have family. In Russia and in America, I have family who love me and want me. Even Saul wants me, in his own way.

For Ilya, there is no family. In America there is an uncle, an uncle who works three jobs and wants Ilya not because he loves him, but because of the money

---

turn my back on forget about

Ilya can earn. Not once since I've been here has the uncle come to visit Ilya. Not once. Is this the way family behaves?

Poor Ilya, he cannot get back his old life in Russia. Ilya's mother **became widowed** when he was two. When she remarried, her new husband did not want Ilya. That is why she sent him to America. Ilya can't go back. At least not to **his own people**. Maybe you and Hannah would take him in. Could you raise a little Russian boy?

No, of course not. You would tell me the wisest thing to do would be to help Ilya prepare for America. He has no choice but to come into America.

He's a smart boy. He knows the poetry of Pushkin **by heart**. I have read to him so often that now he reads **passages** himself.

I tell him, "Ilya, you should be learning to read English, not Russian. You are going to be an American."

---

became widowed lost her husband
his own people his family and friends
by heart without reading it
passages parts

He looks at me with those stormy eyes. Sometimes he looks so lost.

We are trapped between two worlds, Ilya and I. Ilya wants to go back to Russia, to the only place he has ever known. I want to enter America. Yet neither of us can leave this island.

Ilya is eating and **the circles lessen under his eyes**, but still he is thin and frail. I think the doctors and Mr. Fargate **are more concerned with his mind, though, than with his health**.

They think Ilya is a simpleton—because he won't take food for himself. I am still putting food on his plate. And he never talks to anyone else. He talks only to me, when no one is listening. But he is very smart, Tovah. Any seven-year-old who can read Pushkin is one clever boy. I must help him see that his life is

....

the circles lessen under his eyes he looks healthier

are more concerned with his mind, though, than with his health worry that he cannot read or make decisions more than they worry that he is sick here, in America, not back in Russia. How do I do that?

Tovah, you would know.

My dear cousin, I miss you **like soup misses salt**.

Shalom,
Rifka

....

like soup misses salt so much

BEFORE YOU MOVE ON...

1. **Simile** On page 160, Rifka's mother visited. Rifka said her heart would break open like an egg. Why did she make this comparison?

2. **Inference** Reread page 167. Even though we never hear Tovah, how does she help Rifka?

LOOK AHEAD Read pages 170–179 to see how Ilya scares Rifka.

Rifka yells at Ilya for wasting paper. She worries that the people in the hospital will punish them.

. . . Oh, mournful season that delights the eyes,
Your farewell beauty captivates my spirit.
I love the pomp of Nature's fading dyes,
The forests, garmented in gold and purple,
The rush of noisy wind, and the pale skies
Half-hidden by the clouds in darkling billows,
And the rare sun-ray and the early frost,
And threats of grizzled Winter, heard and lost. . . .
—Pushkin

❧

October 14, 1920
Ellis Island

Dear Tovah,

Ilya got me into such trouble today. We were walking through a part of the hospital we didn't know very well. We heard the **d-d-d-d** of a machine. Ilya loves machines. He dragged me over to the place where some men were working on a balcony overlooking the harbor.

I stepped closer to the workmen. One of them used English words I hadn't heard before. I don't think they were words Mama would want me to learn, but still I was curious.

All of a sudden I realized Ilya was missing. He is never more than a step or two away from me. Now for the first time in weeks he had disappeared from my sight.

I rushed toward the balcony, calling for him. A little boy could easily fall over the edge into the water. I ran from the balcony to the hallway, then back again, fretting in Russian. The workmen **stopped their hammers** to stare at me.

It took a moment for the sound of their machines to stop inside my head, but then, in the silence, I heard Ilya's high voice, crying out.

....

d-d-d-d sound
stopped their hammers stopped working

I turned toward the sound. There stood a row of metal toilet stalls. It was from the stalls that Ilya's voice came. Inside one I found him. He had his back to me, and clouds of white paper flew over his head as if some great white bird were descending on him.

But it was no bird. Ilya was unrolling toilet paper, an endless ribbon of it. As he unwound it, he laughed wildly. He cried, "Paper! Paper!"

I scolded him in Russian. I yelled for him to stop.

"Look what you are doing, Ilya. You are going to get us killed. Look how you are wasting the paper."

I grabbed his arm, holding it away, while frantically I started rolling the paper back. I was trying to wind it up so no one would punish us and I was yelling at him in Russian.

One of the workers **started toward** us. He pushed his big arm into the stall past me and Ilya. The worker ripped out the roll of toilet paper, throwing it over the rail and into the harbor. The white tail of Ilya's **unravelings** sailed over our heads and disappeared

---

started toward came near
unravelings loose toilet paper

beyond the balcony.

The worker looked as though he would next **pitch us** into the harbor.

Well, I grabbed Ilya and I ran with him so fast he cracked his shoulder against a wall. I didn't stop to comfort him.

"We're going to get killed!" I cried, pulling him, checking over my shoulder every few seconds to see if the man was chasing us.

"Don't you ever do that again," I told Ilya, trying to catch my breath. We **collapsed** on my cot.

Nurse Bowen came over. Ilya held his shoulder and wept.

"What happened?" the nurse asked, examining Ilya's shoulder.

"Promise you won't tell Mr. Fargate?" I asked. "Promise you won't let him send us back to Russia."

"Tell me, Rifka," the nurse said.

"IIya unrolled toilet paper," I said, believing IIya

....

pitch us throw both of us
collapsed fell

had **committed one of the worst offenses he could ever commit here**.

"Toilet paper?" the nurse asked. "What are you talking about, Rifka?"

I told her about the stalls and the workmen. Nurse Bowen started laughing.

"This is not funny," I told her. "In Russia, to waste paper is a terrible crime."

"Well, in America it's not, Rifka," Nurse Bowen said. "There is plenty of paper. Toilet paper, newspaper, every kind of paper. Don't worry. We're not going to send you back to Russia over a roll of toilet paper."

She told me to tell IIya that his shoulder would be fine. Already he had stopped crying.

Nurse Bowen went away, still laughing.

I felt a little **insulted** that she should laugh at me. But if paper was not so precious here, maybe it was a little funny. Maybe. And maybe I could get some of that plentiful paper Nurse Bowen talked about

....

committed one of the worst offenses he could ever commit here done one of the worst things he could do in America

insulted unhappy

to write on.

Ilya slid the Pushkin out from under my pillow. He handed it to me to read to him.

I said, "No, no Pushkin. I'm going to write a poem of my own."

Remember, Tovah, when I said I might try? Well, I've been writing a little at the back of our book. There is hardly any **room** left between my letters to you and my poetry, but still I keep writing. Sometimes even in English. It is not very good poetry. Mostly, it doesn't rhyme, but I write anyway. I write poems about Russia and Bubbe Ruth and you and Hannah and coming to America and Ellis Island.

I asked Nurse Bowen for some of that paper she was talking about. She gave me a handful.

A handful of paper, Tovah. The paper alone is enough to **draw the words from inside me**. I took the paper and our Pushkin outside. Ilya, of course, followed behind me like a shadow.

It is pretty here on the island. Across the harbor,

....

room space

draw the words from inside me make me think of words to write tall buildings stand like giant guards, blocking my way to Mama and Papa. I fear those guards will never let me pass. Yet even in my fear **I cannot deny the beauty of this place**.

The leaves change color just as they do in Berdichev. Geese fly overhead, honking, forming and reforming in the blue sky above Miss Liberty. The sun feels warm on my shoulders and the smell of autumn tickles my nose.

My writing maybe is not as beautiful as Pushkin's, but it comforts me. Ilya likes it, too. He makes me read my poems over and over to him. It is nice to have an audience.

You didn't know I would **turn out to be** a poet, did you, Tovah? Is that being clever?

Shalom, my cousin,
Rifka

I cannot deny the beauty of this place I think this place is beautiful

turn out to be become

Mr. Fargate is ready to make the decision that will change Ilya's and Rifka's lives. Then Rifka's head starts to itch again.

. . . This heart its leave of you has taken;
Accept, my distant dear, love's close,
As does the wife death leaves forsaken,
As does the exile's comrade, shaken
And mute, who clasps him once, and
goes.
—Pushkin

ॐ

October 21, 1920
Ellis Island

Dear Tovah,

The baby with the typhus, the baby I have taken care of since I got here three weeks ago, I found her in her crib this morning, Tovah. I found her dead.

She died during the night, alone. I remember how her dark eyes would **look straight inside me**. She would hold on to my finger with her tiny fist and squeeze **as if she could squeeze my strength into her**. I gave her my strength, gladly, all that I could give her. It wasn't enough. I loved that little baby, Tovah.

Now Mr. Fargate comes in. He says he has **let my family know** that tomorrow he will decide about my case. So tomorrow I learn what will **become of** me. Mr. Fargate has called Ilya's uncle, too.

I'm so frightened, Tovah. More than an ocean separates me from Berdichev now. Inside me, something has changed. I can't go back.

Worst of all, my head has begun itching again. It started a day or so ago. I am afraid to lift off my scarf and look at it. I couldn't bear to see sores covering my scalp again.

So the ringworm isn't gone after all. If they check, they will send me back for sure.

I should have just remained in Russia as you did,

....

look straight inside me look at me

as if she could squeeze my strength into her so hard as if it could help her live

let my family know told my family

become of happen to

Tovah. That would have been the wisest thing of all. The thought of going back across the ocean, across Europe, through Poland, back to Berdichev . . . it is too much for me to bear.

To leave America without ever having a chance at it, to leave Mama and Papa and all my big brothers when I know how much they need me, I can't let myself think of it.

Even if I could travel all those miles, even if I managed to find my way back, even if the Russians did not kill me, I couldn't live in Berdichev again. I have lived too much in this big world to go back to Berdichev.

Shalom, Tovah,
Rifka

BEFORE YOU MOVE ON...

1. **Character's Motive** Why was Rifka angry at Ilya for wasting toilet paper?

2. **Inference** Rifka's head started itching. How did she feel about this? Why?

LOOK AHEAD What happens when Ilya meets with Mr. Fargate? Read pages 180–190 to find out.

Mr. Fargate and Doctor Askin see Rifka and Ilya again. Ilya reads Pushkin for them. Then he recites some of Rifka's poetry.

. . . The heavy-hanging chains will
fall,
The walls will crumble at a word;
And Freedom greet you in the light,
And brothers give you back the
sword.
—Pushkin

October 22, 1920
Ellis Island

Dear Tovah,

This is the last letter I will ever write you from
Ellis Island. It is almost impossible to believe what has

happened today. **I don't know where to start.**

I woke up feeling **like a lump of wool had caught in my throat.** I let llya sleep in bed beside me last night. I knew it was probably our last night together, whatever happened.

We whispered for a long time in the dark. I told him not to be afraid of America. That he would make friends here. That his uncle would love him and take care of him.

I told him that in Russia, he would always be a peasant. That would never change. He would die young just as his father had and maybe leave a little boy just as his father had left him. I told him in America, he could grow up to be anything he wanted. He could have a wife and children and live to be an old man and see his grandchildren born.

He said he would stay, if he could marry me.

That made me smile. I'm glad it was dark so he couldn't see. I didn't want him to think I was **making fun.**

....

I don't know where to start. I have so much to tell.
like a lump of wool had caught in my throat nervous
making fun laughing at him

I have learned so much about America in these three weeks. It is hard to believe I got so upset over Ilya and the toilet paper just a few days ago. I laugh about it now. I understand so much more.

Yet as I woke this morning, with Ilya curled up beside me, I wondered **what good would come from** my understanding. What chance did I have of staying? Not only did I have no hair, but the ringworm had returned. Every second I had to remind myself not to scratch at the ringworm.

Ilya had America within his grasp, but me, I held nothing. I held only Russia.

Mr. Fargate, the man who makes these decisions, came into the little office beside the ward. He called Ilya in first.

Ilya gripped my hand and pulled me into the office with him. Mr. Fargate and Doctor Askin discussed Ilya, examined him. Mr. Fargate noticed that Ilya had gained weight.

Ilya's uncle sat in a chair nearby. He was such a

....

what good would come from whether anything good would happen because of

Ilya had America within his grasp It would be easy for Ilya to become an American if he tried little man, with thin blond hair and stormy eyes, just like Ilya's.

My family, my whole beautiful family, Papa and Mama and Saul, and Nathan and Asher and Reuben, and Isaac and Sadie and the little baby, Aaron, they were all there, too. How I longed to be with them. I looked at each of them, **memorizing their faces**. My brothers Reuben and Asher and Isaac, I would have known them anywhere. Isaac and Asher look just like Papa, and Reuben, he looks like me. When they first arrived, I hugged and kissed them all.

I whispered to Saul, "Did you get the candlesticks?"

He said, "Yes, Rifka. But I have not given them to Mama yet."

"What are you waiting for?" I asked.

Saul shrugged.

Now I could only look at my family from a distance. Ilya needed me.

Ilya's uncle **cowered under the giant shadow of**

....

memorizing their faces trying to remember their faces
cowered under the giant shadow of looked small next to

my family. When Nurse Bowen passed him, his hair lifted off his high forehead in the little breeze that she made. He held his hat in his hand, his fingers inching around the brim over and over again, his shoulders hunched. It looked to me like he needed Ilya as much as Ilya needed him.

Mr. Fargate said, "This boy shows **minimal** intelligence. He doesn't feed himself, he doesn't speak. Has there been any change since his last review, Doctor Askin?"

The doctor said many things, but the more he talked the more clear it became he didn't know Ilya at all.

He believed Ilya *was* a simpleton.

Ilya could read Pushkin. He was smart enough to **figure out** if he starved himself, he'd get shipped back home. That's not a simpleton. They couldn't send him back for being a simpleton.

Mr. Fargate pushed his glasses up on his nose and leaned over his desk to **peer** at Ilya.

....

minimal very little
figure out know that
peer look closely

"Can you speak?" he asked in English.

Ilya stared straight into Mr. Fargate's eyes, but he said nothing.

"He doesn't understand English," Nurse Bowen said.

Mr. Fargate nodded. "Find someone who can translate."

"I can," I offered.

Mr. Fargate looked over his glasses at me. "Ask the boy if he can talk," said Mr. Fargate.

"Talk," I told Ilya in Russian.

Ilya glared at me.

"Ilya, talk!"

Ilya slowly shook his head.

"Go get my Pushkin," I told Ilya.

He looked up at me and brushed his blond hair out of his eyes. His uncle looked up at me, too, **startled**.

"Go on, get the book," I repeated.

Ilya was being as stubborn as ever. He stood in his place and **refused to move**.

....

startled surprised
refused to move would not move

"Ilya." I commanded. "Go over there and get the book of Pushkin. Now!"

I pointed toward my cot.

Ilya stared at me with those stormy green eyes. Then he lowered his chin, brushed past his uncle, and got the book.

"Ilya is a smart boy," I told Mr. Fargate in English.

I looked down at Ilya. "Read to them," I ordered in Russian. "Show them that you are smart enough to live in America. I know how clever you are, Ilya. But Mr. Fargate needs to know. Your uncle needs to know, too."

I looked back to where the uncle sat with his hat in his lap. The man's eyes never left Ilya. He **drank in the sight of his nephew the way a thirsty man pulls at a dipper of water**.

Still, Ilya remained silent.

Mr. Fargate lifted the stamp, the **deportation stamp**.

....

drank in the sight of his nephew the way a thirsty man pulls at a dipper of water was very happy to see Ilya

deportation stamp stamp to send Ilya back to Russia

"Please," I begged Ilya's uncle in Russian. "You are losing him. He must prove to them that he is not a simpleton or they will send him away."

I tried to get the uncle to understand.

"He is afraid of you. He thinks you don't want him."

"He is my sister's son," Ilya's uncle said in Russian. "Of course I want him. He is my **flesh and blood**. I sent for him to give him a better life here in America. I work day and night so he can have a good life."

"Do you hear, Ilya?" I said. "Do you hear?"

Ilya turned his eyes for the first time on his uncle.

"Doctor Askin," I said in English. "Ilya is not a simpleton. I know he won't talk to you. But he *can* talk. He can read, too. He is only seven years, but he can read."

I gave Ilya the book. "Now read," I commanded in Russian.

Ilya's uncle got up out of his seat and came over. He put his hat down on the edge of Mr. Fargate's desk

---

flesh and blood family

and **knelt before** his nephew. "Please, Ilya," he said. "Do what your friend says."

Ilya brushed the blond hair up onto his forehead. Then he began to read.

> "*Storm-clouds dim the sky; the tempest*
> *Weaves the snow in patterns wild . . .*"

Ilya's voice shook, but he was reading.

> "*Like a beast the **gale** is howling,*
> *And now wailing like a child . . .*"

Tears filled the eyes of Ilya's uncle.

"Is he reading?" Mr. Fargate asked. "Is that Russian?"

Ilya's uncle nodded. "Pushkin."

"Let me see the book a moment," Mr. Fargate said. He reached for the Pushkin. Ilya pulled it back, clasping the book to his chest.

"Show Mr. Fargate the book," I said in Russian.

....

knelt before went down on his knees in front of

gale wind

"Go on, Ilya."

Ilya's hands trembled as he handed the book to Mr. Fargate. Mr. Fargate opened our Pushkin to another page. "Read this."

*". . . I like the grapes whose **clusters ripen**
Upon the hillside in the sun . . ."*

Ilya's finger **dragged across** the page as he read the words.

I smiled. Doctor Askin smiled. Nurse Bowen smiled, too.

"He understands this?" Mr. Fargate said. "At the age of seven?"

"Yes, sir," I said. "He understands."

Mr. Fargate lifted the stamp that permitted Ilya to enter the country and **thumped** it down on Ilya's papers. Ilya was going to stay in America.

"Did I do it right, Rifka?" he asked in Russian.

"Yes, Ilya," I said. "You did it just right."

---

clusters ripen *bunches become ready to eat*
dragged across pointed to
thumped pushed

Ilya's uncle still knelt on the floor beside us. His arms opened up to take Ilya in. Oh, Tovah. You should have seen the way Ilya and his uncle **embraced**. In all the times he clung to me, Ilya never held me in such a way. Never.

....

embraced hugged

BEFORE YOU MOVE ON...

1. **Summarize** Reread pages 184–186. Why did Mr. Fargate almost send Ilya back to Russia?

2. **Cause and Effect** What happened that made Ilya read?

LOOK AHEAD Is it better to be beautiful or clever? Read to page 203 to find out what Rifka thinks.

Ilya had attracted a lot of attention on the ward.
No one but myself had ever heard his voice. Now
there he was, reading Pushkin. Other nurses and
doctors came over. They stood around **in wonder** at
Ilya, now jabbering in Russian as he led his uncle back
to his cot.

I could not listen to what they were saying. The
time had come for my review. My family waited
tensely, some sitting, some standing, waiting for a
decision about me. If only I could melt into their tight
strong circle, but now, as I had so often over the last
year, I stood alone.

Mr. Fargate was talking with Doctor Askin about
me. He wanted to know about the ringworm.

"She arrived fully cured," Doctor Askin said.
"They made sure she **was clean** in Belgium before
they sent her."

Please, I prayed. Don't let them check for the
ringworm now.

They hadn't checked in over a week. I'd

Ilya had attracted a lot of attention on the ward. A lot of
people in the ward came to watch Ilya.

in wonder very surprised

was clean was healthy; had no diseases

shown no sign of being infectious for so long, they believed the ringworm was gone.

I bit the insides of my cheeks to keep from scratching my itchy scalp. In my head, I repeated Sister Katrina's prayer; I repeated a few Hebrew prayers, too.

Mr. Fargate turned to Doctor Askin. "What about her hair? **Is there any sign of growth?**"

I slipped my hand up to my kerchief and gave a quick scratch. I tried not to, but I couldn't keep my hand away from it. It itched so badly. It had been itching all morning.

"Here, Rifka," Doctor Askin said kindly, starting to unknot my kerchief. "Let me look once more to see if there is any sign of hair."

I pulled away.

Oh, Tovah, if ever I needed to be clever, it was now.

"You know," I said. "What does it matter if my hair grows? A girl cannot depend on her looks. It is

....

Is there any sign of growth? Has her hair grown?

better to be clever. I learned to speak English in three weeks, you know."

"Yes, I know," Mr. Fargate replied.

"I help here, too," I said. "I am a good worker."

Mr. Fargate's eyeglasses slid down to the tip of his nose and he stared over them at me. "Not very modest, is she?"

They all laughed.

"It is true!" I cried. "I *am* a good worker!"

"You are, Rifka," Doctor Askin agreed. He turned to Mr. Fargate. "With the right opportunity, the girl could study medicine. She has skill and talent."

"In your opinion, then," Mr. Fargate said, "she would not end up a **ward of the state**?"

"Who can tell?" said the doctor. "But the opposite is more likely. I have seen her care for the patients. Compassion is a part of medicine you can't teach, Mr. Fargate. **Compassion** is a quality I have often seen in Rifka. Look what she did for the boy."

"I still worry about her hair," Mr. Fargate said.

....

ward of the state person the government has to take care of
Compassion Kindness to other people

I looked Mr. Fargate right in the eye. "I do not need hair to get a good life," I said.

"Maybe right now you don't," Mr. Fargate answered. "But what about when you wish to marry?"

"If I wish to marry, Mr. Fargate," I said—can you believe I spoke like this to an American official, Tovah?— "if I wish to marry, I will do so with hair or without hair."

I heard Mama gasp. This much English she understood.

Mr. Fargate leaned forward **to study me**. He stared at me through the glasses balanced at the bottom of his nose.

"You have plenty to say, young lady," Mr. Fargate said.

"Yes," I agreed, "I do."

"Oy, Rifka," Mama whispered.

I turned toward Mama. What I saw, though, was my brother Saul kneeling beside Ilya. Ilya and Saul were looking at the book of Pushkin together. Then

....

to study me and looked at me closely

194

Saul stood and took Ilya's hand and they approached Mr. Fargate.

"Yes?" Mr. Fargate asked.

Ilya looked up at me. "Read to them," he commanded in Russian.

"Ilya, that will not work for me," I told him in his own language. "They already know I can read. My **case** is not the same as yours."

"Read to them your poetry," Saul said. "The words you have written in the back of this book."

I looked hard at Ilya. "You **had no right to show** that to anyone," I said. "Those are my words."

"They are good words, Rifka," Saul said.

"They are nothing," I answered. "Simple little poems. They don't even rhyme. What good would it do to read such things aloud? Leave it be."

Ilya would not leave it.

He took the Pushkin and **elbowed** in front of me to stand under the stern eye of Mr. Fargate.

"This," he said, speaking English with a very thick

....

case problem
had no right to show should not have shown
elbowed pushed

accent. "This Rifka write."

I'd never heard him speak anything but Russian before.

He took a deep breath and let it out. He swallowed once, hard. Then he began **reciting** my latest poem in English. How I had struggled with the words. Ilya had made me repeat them to him each time I stopped or changed something. Now he remembered it perfectly. He didn't look at the book. He just held it in front of him and said the poem from memory.

> *"I leave to you the low and leaning room,*
> *where once we drank the honey-sweetened tea,*
> *and bowed our heads in prayer and waited there,*
> *for cossacks with their boots and bayonets."*

They were all listening, even Ilya's uncle.

> *"I leave behind my cousins, young and dear;*
> *They'll never know the freedom I have known,*

....

reciting saying

*Or learn as I have learned, that kindness **dwells**,*
In hearts that have no fear."

"You wrote these words?" Mr. Fargate asked.

I nodded, embarrassed.

"Rifka Nebrot," Mr. Fargate said. "This is a very nice poem."

"You think?" I asked. "That is just one poem." I took the book from Ilya and started turning pages. "I have more, Mr. Fargate, many more. I can read to you. Do you have time? Here is one you will like, I think . . . "

Mr. Fargate looked at his watch. Then he looked at Doctor Askin. "No wonder the boy never talked. She talks enough for both of them."

Now, I thought, it would be clever to keep quiet.

"Well, Miss Nebrot," Mr. Fargate said. "After **giving the matter some consideration**, I think you are correct. Whether you wish to marry or not is **no business of mine**." He turned to Doctor Askin.

....

dwells lives

giving the matter some consideration thinking about it

no business of mine not something for me to worry about

"Heaven help the man she does marry."

Turning back to me, he said, "I have no doubt that if you wish to marry, you will manage to do so, whether you have hair or not."

Then he looked over to Mama and Papa. "Mr. and Mrs. Nebrot. These are your daughter's papers. With this stamp I give permission for her to enter the United States of America."

My heart **thundered** in my chest.

Mr. Fargate stamped my entrance papers and handed them to me. "Here, Rifka Nebrot," he said. "Welcome to America."

The nurses and doctors **swept over me**. Ilya, too. Best of all my family, my beloved family, Saul, Nathan, Reuben, Asher, Isaac, Mama, Papa, Sadie, and little Aaron. **There was such a commotion** with all the kissing and the hugging I could hardly breathe.

Then I felt something that made me stiffen with fear. In all the kissing and hugging, someone had loosened the kerchief covering my head. I felt it

....

thundered beat loudly

swept over me hugged me

There was such a commotion People were so excited

slipping off.

I tried to get my hand up to hold on to it, but Doctor Askin held my arms. He enfolded me in a crushing hug, and I felt the kerchief sliding down, inching away from the sores it covered, to **betray me**. The kerchief, as Doctor Askin let go, dropped around my neck, settling on my shoulders like a heavy weight.

With my head exposed to the air, it itched worse than ever.

Quickly my hands flew up to replace the kerchief. I swept it back up in a matter of seconds, trying to cover my head before anyone had a chance to see my scalp.

I wasn't fast enough. **Towering over me as he did**, Saul had seen it. Doctor Askin had seen it, too. They stared down at me.

"Rifka, your head," Saul said.

I pulled the kerchief tightly over my scalp.

Not now, I prayed. They've stamped the papers.

....

betray me show my secret
Towering over me as he did Since he was so tall

Don't let them find out now.

"But Rifka," Saul said. "There's something on your head."

"Take off your kerchief," Doctor Askin ordered.

"Please," I begged in a whisper. "Don't make me take it off."

"Take it off, Rifka," Doctor Askin insisted.

My hands shook as I lifted them to the knot under my chin. I had difficulty untying it. Everyone stared at me, at my trembling hands, at my **disloyal kerchief.**

"Whatever it is," I said, trying to talk my way out of it, "I'm certain it will go away."

I could delay no longer. The kerchief dropped to my shoulders.

"This isn't going away," said Nurse Bowen. "Here, feel for yourself."

She took my hand and **guided it up to the top** of my head. I stretched my hand out, expecting to feel the ringworm sores under my fingertips.

....

disloyal kerchief kerchief that did not stay on my head
guided it up to the top put it on top

But I didn't feel ringworm.

I felt hair!

Not very much. But it was hair. My hair! And it was growing.

₰ ₰ ₰

Mama and Papa are sitting beside me on a bench at Ellis Island. We are waiting for my brother Isaac. I am writing on the paper Nurse Bowen gave to me.

Saul says at home there is a notebook full of paper, a whole empty notebook for me to write in. He bought it for me himself, with his own money. And at home is a pair of brass candlesticks, he said. A pair just like the ones Mama used to own. Tonight, Saul said, tonight I would give them to her.

On my head is the black velvet hat with the shirring and the light blue lining. My head still itches, but Nurse Bowen said that is normal. That often the scalp **prickles** when new hair grows in.

....

prickles itches

Mama's gold locket lies softly between her breasts again, where it belongs. Around my neck is a small Star of David on a silver chain, a gift from Mama and Papa.

"Saul said this is what you would like the most," Mama had said when she gave it to me.

"Saul was right," I said, and I kissed Mama and Papa on their hands, first one and then the other.

My brother Isaac has gone home to Borough Park to bring his car. He said, "**Never mind** the trouble, my sister Rifka is going to enter America in style."

A clever girl like me, Tovah, how else should I enter America?

I will write you tonight a real letter, a letter I can send. I will wrap up our precious book and send it to you, too, so you will know of my journey. I hope you can read all the tiny words squeezed onto the **worn** pages. I hope they bring to you the comfort they have

....

Never mind Do not worry about
worn old, used

brought to me. I send you my love, Tovah. At last I send you my love from America.

Shalom, my dear cousin,
Rifka

BEFORE YOU MOVE ON...

1. **Plot** Reread pages 192–193. What lesson did Rifka learn?

2. **Character** How did Rifka use the lesson to convince Mr. Fargate that she didn't need hair?

LOOK AHEAD Read the Historical Note to see what was happening in Russia at the time Rifka's story happened.

Historical Note

In the years surrounding World War I, many people living in Eastern Europe found it difficult to feed and clothe their families. **War made supplies short** and conditions were often intolerable. National borders shifted back and forth, splitting families apart, increasing their suffering. These struggles led to frustration and anger.

The impoverished peasants of Russia endured great hardships **while the government far above them crumbled with the ousting of the czar.** To ease the mounting pressure, the government placed agents in the villages and towns of Russia. These agents intentionally stirred up trouble, diverting the peasants' anger away from the government and directing it toward the Jews. Peasants, **infected with a mob fever** that produced the pogroms, swept through Jewish settlements breaking windows, looting,

....

War made supplies short There was little food

while the government far above them crumbled with the ousting of the czar when the government changed leadership

infected with a mob fever became a group of angry people burning, beating, and murdering the unfortunates in their path.

During this period in Russian history, many **restrictions were borne on the shoulders of** the Jewish people. They were denied the right to earn a living at most professions. Travel beyond their **ghettos or settlements** was forbidden without proper government paperwork, which was often either slow in coming or denied altogether. Jews could not own property, nor were they allowed to have in their possession more than two of any given object.

Many Russians **sought to drive** Jews from the country permanently by making their lives wretched. In the Russian Army, Jewish boys were assigned the least desirable tasks. Often, if they survived the **perils** of their assignments, if they survived the inadequate provisions supplied them, they were tortured or killed by their own comrades, the non-Jewish soldiers they served beside.

....

restrictions were borne on the shoulders of things were taken away from

ghettos or settlements villages

sought to drive tried to move

perils dangers

This climate drove thousands and thousands of families from their homelands—not just Jews, but many others as well. In search of a better life, those families **sought sanctuary** in countries across the globe. We, today, **are the beneficiaries of their legacy of** courage and determination.

....

sought sanctuary looked for safety

are the beneficiaries of their legacy of enjoy better lives because of their

BEFORE YOU MOVE ON...

1. **Author's Purpose** Why did the author include a historical note?

2. **Summarize** Why was life so difficult for Jewish people in the years around World War I?